The Ponytail Girls

A Roller Coaster Year

Owner

Ayanna

LEGACY PRESS®

Other books in the Ponytail Girls series:

Book 1
Meet the Ponytail Girls

Book 2
The Impossible Christmas Present

Book 3
Lost on Monster Mountain

Book 4
A Stormy Spring

Book 5
Escape From Camp Porcupine

Book 6
What's Up With Her?

The Ponytail Girls

A Roller Coaster Year

Bonnie Compton Hanson

Dedication

To all the Ponytail Girls who love God
and want to live for Him.

THE PONYTAIL GIRLS/BOOK 7: A ROLLER COASTER YEAR
© 2009 by Legacy Press
ISBN 10: 1-58411-085-6
ISBN 13: 978-1-58411-085-9
Legacy reorder# LP48047
JUVENILE FICTION / Religious / Christian

Legacy Press
P.O. Box 261129
San Diego, CA 92196

Cover Illustrator: Terry Julien
Interior Illustrator: Aline Heiser

Scriptures are from the *Holy Bible: New International Version* (North
American Edition), ©1973, 1978, 1984 by the International Bible Society.
Used by permission of Zondervan Bible Publishers.

Printed in the United States of America

Contents

~ Introduction ~

Welcome to the *Ponytail Girls!* Whether you wear a ponytail or not, you can share in the adventures of Sam Pearson and her friends, the PTs (that's short for Ponytails.) Just like you, the PTs love sports and shopping and fun with their friends at school.

The PTs also want to live in a way that is pleasing to God. So when they have problems and conflicts, they look to God and His Word, the Bible. They also seek help from their parents, their pastor, or their Sunday school class teacher, just as you do.

Each chapter in this book presents a new problem for the PTs to solve. In addition, there is a Bible story to help explain the Christian value that they learned. A Bible memory verse is included for you to practice and share.

There may be words in this book that are new to you, especially some Bible names and Spanish words. Look them up in the Glossary at the end of the book, then use the syllables to sound out the words.

In addition to the stories, each chapter includes questions to answer as well as fun quizzes, puzzles, and other activities. Also, at the end of each chapter you will get a clue that leads to finishing the "Greatest

Show on Earth" puzzle on page 27. Remember to fill in the puzzle each time so you can see its secret message at the end! The answers to all the puzzles (not that you'll need them) are at the end of the book.

The first *Ponytail Girls* book, *Meet the Ponytail Girls*, begins just before school starts in the fall. In *The Impossible Christmas Present*, you will follow the PTs through the tragedies and triumphs of their holiday season. *Lost on Monster Mountain* sees the PTs off to Winter Camp with their Madison classmates. *A Stormy Spring* follows the PTs' adventures after returning from camp. *Escape from Camp Porcupine* takes them back to camp—this time in the summer. *What's Up With Her?* explores all the joys and problems of a teen-and-tween talent show. Right now, get ready for more fun with your PT friends in *A Roller Coaster Year*.

The fun doesn't end with the stories. You can start your own Ponytail Girls Club. You can join by yourself, of course, but it's so much more fun if one of your friends joins with you. Or even five or six of them! There is no cost. You can read the *Ponytail Girls* stories together, do the puzzles and other activities, study the Bible stories, and learn the Bible verses.

If your friends have their own *Ponytail Girls* books, each girl can write in her own copy at the same time. Arrange a regular meeting time and place, and plan to do special things together just as the PTs do in the stories, such as shopping, Bible study, homework, or helping others.

Meet Your Ponytail Girls!

· WHO ARE THEY? ·

The Ponytail Girls are middle school friends who enjoy school, church, shopping, and being with their friends and families. They also love meeting new friends. Friends just like you! You'll love being a part of their lives.

The PTs all attend Madison Middle School in the small town of Circleville. They're all also members of Miss Kotter's Sunday school class at nearby Faith Church on Sunday mornings. On Sunday evenings, they attend the special Zone 56 youth group for guys and girls their age. Their pastor is Rev. J. T. McConahan, and their youth leader is Pastor Andrew Garretti, also known as "Pastor Andy."

Sam and Sara grew up in Circleville. Le's and LaToya's families moved into their neighborhood last year. When Sam and Sara met them at school, they invited them to church. Then Maria moved to Circleville and she became a PT, followed by Jenna and Brittany and Sonya. Now it would be hard for all of them to imagine not being PTs.

How did the PTs get their club name? Well, as you can see from their pictures, they all wear ponytails of one kind or another. So that's what their other friends started calling them just for fun. Then one day LaToya shortened it to "PTs." Now that's what they all call themselves.

The PTs' club meetings are held whenever they can all get together. The girls have a secret motto: PT4JC, which means "Ponytails for Jesus Christ." They also have a secret code for the club's name: a "P" and a "T" back to back. But most of the time they don't want to keep secrets. They want to share with everyone the Good News about their best friend, Jesus.

Have fun sharing in the PTs' adventures. Laugh with them in their silly times, think and pray with them through their problems, and learn with them that the answers to all problems can be found right in God's Word. Keep your Bible and a sharpened pencil handy. Sam and the others are waiting for you!

GET TO KNOW THE PTs

Sam Pearson *has a long blond ponytail, sparkling blue eyes and a dream: she wants to play professional basketball. She also likes to design clothes. Sam's name is really "Samantha," but her friends and family just call her "Sam" for short. Her little brother is Petie. Joe, her dad, is great at fixing things, like cars and bikes, and he runs the Superservice Auto car repair shop. Her mom, Jean, bakes scrumptious goodies and works at the Paws and Pooches Animal Shelter. Sneezit is the family tiny dog and Sunlight their kitten.*

LaToya Thomas' *black curls are ponytailed high above her ears. That way she doesn't miss a thing going on! LaToya's into gymnastics and playing the guitar. Her big sister, Tina, is a nurse. Her mom is a school teacher; her dad works with Mr. Pearson at Superservice. Also living with the Thomases is LaToya's beloved, wheelchair-bound grandmother, Granny B, and the family kitten, Twilight.*

Le Tran *parts her glossy black hair to one side, holding it back with one small ponytail. She loves sewing, soccer, and playing the violin. Her mother, Viola, a concert pianist, often plays duets with her. Her father died in an accident, but became a Christian before he died. Le's mother is a new Christian. She is engaged to marry Dr. Phan, music director at a Vietnamese church. He's a widower with two little boys, Michael and Nicolas. Le's kitten is Midnight.*

• Le Tran •

Sara Fields *lives down the street from Sam. She keeps her fiery red hair from flying away by tying it into ponytails flat against each side of her head. Sara has freckles, glasses, and a great sense of humor. She loves singing, softball, ice skating, and cheerleading. Sara has a big brother, Tony, and a big dog, Tank, plus a kitten, Stormy. Her parents, Bob and Betsy, are artists.*

• Sara Fields •

When **Maria Moreno** *moved in next door to Sam, she quickly became a PT, too. Maria pulls part of her long, brown hair into one topknot ponytail at the back; the rest hangs loose. She is tall, the way basketball-lover Sam would like to be. But Maria's into science and tennis, not basketball. At home, she helps her mother take care of her twin brothers, Juan and Ricardo, her little sister, Lolita, and her kitten, Dinah-Mite. The Morenos all speak both English and Spanish.*

Jenna Jenkins *is tall and wears her rich auburn ponytail high on her head, like a crown. Jenna loves ballet and tennis, her little sister Katie, and twin baby sisters, Noel and Holly, who were born at Christmas. Jenna's mom makes delicious cookies, and her dad is an accountant. Jenna's kitten is Skeeter Bite.*

•Sonya Silverhorse•

Sonya Silverhorse *has a wheelchair and a warm smile. Her bouncy cocker spaniel's name is Cocky, and her kitten is Snow White. Sonya wears her coal-black ponytail long and braided, in honor of her Cherokee background. Her dad is Mr. Pearson's and Mr. Moreno's boss. Her mother died in the same accident that disabled Sonya. But Sonya loves to do things — like wheelchair basketball and playing the harmonica.*

•Brittany Boorsma•

Though **Brittany Boorsma**, *Madison's head cheerleader, was the prettiest girl at school, she was also the most spiteful one—until she invited Christ into her heart. She pulls her long, naturally wavy blond hair together into a ponytail at her shoulder. Last winter she almost died in a blizzard. But God helped two dogs rescue her, and now Hope and Sweet Dreams are part of her family, too. Brittany plays the keyboard. Her father is an insurance agent.*

16

Angie Andrews *is new in town, with a mother who has been quite sick and a father who was stationed overseas. Shy and short, she wears a tiny ponytail in her long brown hair swept off to the side with beads braided in it. She loves to draw and to help people.*

· Angie Andrews ·

Lilia Lancaster, *with her long, firecracker-red, naturally curly ponytail, lives with her family on the McAfee Farms. Her pets are Cocky the rooster and Rocky the hen. Lilia loves music and animals.*

· Lilia Lancaster ·

Miss Kitty Kotter, the girls' Sunday school teacher, is not a PT, but she is an important part of their lives both in church and out of church. Miss Kotter works as a computer engineer. She also loves to go on hikes. Miss Kotter calls the Bible her "how-to book" because, she says, it tells "how to" live. Miss Kotter volunteers at the Circleville Rescue Mission. An orphan, she is especially close to Ma Jones, an old woman who now lives at Whispering Pines Nursing Home.

Get ready to have fun with the PTs!

Chapter 1

"Endless Summer"

Sam looked around at her bedroom in disgust. "Just great! This room is so totally lame!"

Why in the world did she ever ask her Dad to paint it this shade of pink? She needed a new color. Or maybe some really bright posters. Anything but her stupid teddy bears piled everywhere!

Yes, her room was looking pretty lame. And summer wasn't starting out so great either. Especially with no air conditioning. It was hot, hot, HOT! Her blond ponytail drooped down her back in a mess. The rest of her felt as bad as her hair looked.

She stomped into the kitchen. Her little brother Petie was there, stretched out on the floor with their wiener dog, Sneezit, in front of a fan.

"It's like a sauna in here!" Sam complained.

Petie grinned. "I'm cool. Why don't you pour yourself some lemonade so you can be cool, too? Better add some extra sugar, though. You sound kinda sour today!"

"I don't want stupid lemonade." Sam slumped onto the couch. "I just want this lousy summer to be over so it can be cool again and we can do something fun."

"Well, lying here is fun," Petie said, as he rolled onto his back. "On the other hand, I'd love to be getting a new videogame. Or playing with Sneezit down at the Bark Park. Or going swimming at the Circleville City pool. But Mom's not here for us to ask permission to leave the house."

Just then Maria stopped by from next door. "When is it going to cool down?" she asked, grabbing a napkin to wipe the perspiration off her face. "It's too hot to play tennis or anything fun. I just talked to the other PTs and they're all bored, too. Jenna's tired of babysitting her little sister and the twins. Sonya misses her basketball team. At our house, Lolita and the boys are just sitting around watching TV and arguing. Even Le's getting tired of practicing her violin. There's just nothing fun to do around here in the summer."

Petie sat up. "Hey, I see something fun," he said, pointing to the back yard. "Why don't we fill up our little wading pool and splash around in it? It wouldn't cost anything. Mom's already said we could do it whenever we want, as long as we're careful and clean up afterwards."

Sam and Maria looked at each other. "Good thinking, Petie," Sam said. "Maria, you and LaToya have pools. What if we get them all together in our back yard and fill them all up and invite all the kids? We could ask Granny B to help us watch them. That way they could all get cool and we would be cool, too."

"Yea!" Pete cried. "And have lemonade and cookies, too. I'm going to get my swim trunks on right now!"

"Sounds sun-sational!" Maria grinned. "Let's call everyone and do it! Remeber the towels and sunscreen!"

There was soon so much splashing going on in Sam's back yard it might as well have been raining. Even Sneezit joined in the fun.

So did Granny B and Sonya. They both rolled their wheelchairs right up to one of the pools, took off their shoes, and stuck in their bare feet. Granny B grinned. "Now this is living!" she said to the group. "Ain't God good?"

Sam wiggled her toes in the water. Hey, maybe she and Maria could go swimming down at the Shawnee Park pool tomorrow. They could get the whole PT gang there. Or even all the Zone 56ers for another big Splash Bash. And the big County Fair would be coming up soon, too! She could already taste the cotton candy!

"Sure, God's good," she said. "I just love summer. Want to pass the sunscreen—and the corn chips?"

· Good News ·
from God's Word

Sometimes we get bored with everything being the same and we wish things would change. Yet when they do change, we get scared and wish things could be back the way they were. Today's Bible story is about two women who learned that God could bless them wherever they were.

Serah and Dinah Go to Egypt
From Genesis 45-47

Many people have heard about the twelve tribes of Israel, named after the twelve sons of Jacob, who was also called Israel. But did you know that these twelve brothers also had a sister? Her name was Dinah. And one of the brothers, Asher, also had a daughter. Her name was Serah. But most of Jacob's grandchildren were boys, just as most of his children were. So Dinah and Serah were glad to have each other for company!

The land where they were born and grew up was called Canaan in those days. Today it is called Israel. God had promised the land of Israel to Jacob's grandfather, Abraham. So Dinah and Serah were thrilled to grow up there.

Then one day God called them all to move to Egypt because of a big famine. There wouldn't be enough food for the family to eat. One of Jacob's sons, Joseph, already lived there. God promised them they would have a good place to live in Egypt, plenty to eat, and everything they wanted. Still, it was scary to move away from their home.

But God had blessed them back in Israel. And He promised to bless them in Egypt, as well. And He did. Aren't you glad for God's love and blessings?

 ## A Verse to Remember

*"Now, our God, we give you thanks,
and praise your glorious name."*

–1 Chronicles 29:13

Give Sam's Room a New Look

Sam's getting tired of her all-pink room. Can you redecorate her room using the same furniture but with fresh new colors and accessories? You can even include wallpaper designs if you wish.

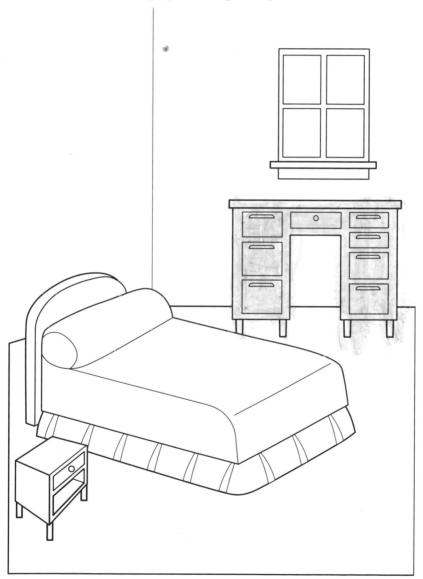

The Greatest Show on Earth Puzzle

Many people love to go to county and state fairs. Sometimes there will be a big sign on the tent saying: "The Greatest Show on Earth." This puzzle has that—and more. It's about something God wants YOU to show! To solve this puzzle, write in the blanks the Secret Letters you will find at the end of each chapter in this book. For this chapter, write the letter "O" for "Open to God's Blessings" in space 2. The final solution is given in the answer key at the end of this book.

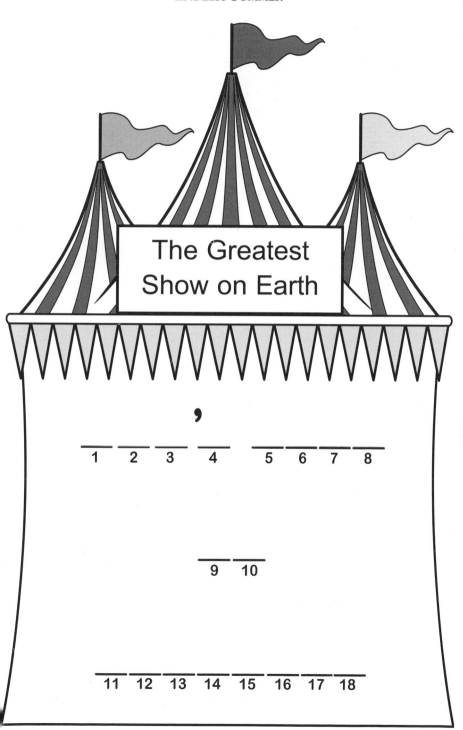

The Greatest
Show on Earth

,

$\overline{}_{1}\ \overline{}_{2}\ \overline{}_{3}\ \overline{}_{4}\quad \overline{}_{5}\ \overline{}_{6}\ \overline{}_{7}\ \overline{}_{8}$

$\overline{}_{9}\ \overline{}_{10}$

$\overline{}_{11}\ \overline{}_{12}\ \overline{}_{13}\ \overline{}_{14}\ \overline{}_{15}\ \overline{}_{16}\ \overline{}_{17}\ \overline{}_{18}$

Chapter 2

Cocky and Rocky

When Pastor Andy held up his hands at their church youth meeting the next Sunday evening, all the kids quieted down. "See these?" he asked.

Ryan looked puzzled. "You mean your *hands*?"

"Yep. Can you think of something they're good for?"

LeToya giggled. "For playing the guitar, doing dishes, digging in the garden, playing videogames, petting a cat, writing a letter, shaking hands, doing high-fives. Just about anything, right?"

"Like swimming!" Sam added. "Or making stuff to enter into the County Fair."

"That's right. But only if we're willing to use them. That's why all the church youth groups in town are getting together for a "willing hands" work day next Saturday." He shrugged. "Should be a lot of fun."

"A work day!" moaned Tyler. "Doesn't sound much like fun to me."

"Well, of course it's not just for fun. Remember the new meeting hall out at McAfee Farms? And how the people's homes were all flooded out and replaced with mobile homes? Well, we're going to go back out there and plant flowers and grass and put in walkways and make everything beautiful around all those new buildings. Afterwards, we'll have a big barnstorming concert right in the barn—with kids from all the churches invited to participate."

"Ooo!" LaToya bounced up in her seat. "Sounds perfect for our Toot 'n Granny Band—the one we played in for the big talent show. But wouldn't we be too worn out to play after all that work? Not to mention starved!"

Their youth pastor laughed. "Don't worry, we'll have food: hot dogs, barbecue beans, potato salad, chips, and pie, with lots of lemonade and iced tea. A real picnic. Okay, who wants to sign up to help?"

Everyone did, of course—that is, everyone who was there. Brittany had left to visit her cousin in Florida. Sonya and her dad were on vacation visiting the Cherokee Nation in Oklahoma. "I'm even going to volunteer my Dad," Angie said. "Now that he's discharged from the Army, he seems depressed and not sure what to do. And he's embarrassed about having an artificial hand. Maybe if he saw how he could encourage the migrant workers he would feel better about things."

When Saturday came, what a workday it turned out to be! There were kids from all the churches in town, even from the Rescue Mission. All of them worked together to show God's love.

Angie's dad wasn't sure he belonged there because he wasn't used to having just one hand. But he had grown up on a farm, and he soon felt right at home. He even made friends with Lilia Lancaster's rooster Cocky, and with Cocky's new friend, Rocky—a beautiful red hen. Rocky loved to sing, just like Cocky.

After the picnic, when everyone piled into the barn with their drums and guitars to perform on a stage made of hay bales, Rocky and Cocky went right along. So did the farm supervisor's dog, Pooch. Pretty soon Max the mule got into the act too. That really brought the house down!

Then Pastor Andy and one of the other pastors told about their missions trip to Peru. After Pastor Andy explained the Gospel, both Angie and her Dad raised their hands to say they wanted to accept Jesus as their own personal Savior.

At last everyone held hands and sang "Amazing Grace," and hugged each other. "I'm so glad we were willing to use our hands for God," LaToya said.

"Awwkk!" Cocky crowed as if to say, "Wait a minute. Some of us didn't use hands—we used claws."

Sam gave him a good petting. "Okay, boy," she said, "the County Fair's coming up soon. Want to enter a contest there with me?"

But Cocky looked over at Rocky. Lilia giggled. "Only if Rocky can enter, too!" she said with a laugh.

· Good News · from God's Word

Angie's father wasn't sure if he'd be able to help with the others. But God can always use our best if we ask Him to help us. Here are some women who gave their best — and helped build God's House.

Rejoicing in What God Has Done
NEHEMIAH 12, 13

Far away from Israel, God's people longed for home. Nebuchadnezzar [*neb-u-chad-nez-zar*], the Babylonian Emperor, had captured them and taken them far away to what is present-day Iraq. After several years, the Babylonian Empire was replaced with a new one—the Persian Empire, centered in what is today called Iran. The new Emperor told God's people they could now go home.

A great crowd of God's people did return to Jerusalem. They rebuilt the Temple that the Babylonians had destroyed. But there was one problem. The city wall was still broken down, so the people didn't feel safe in case of another attack.

Then Nehemiah [*nee-he-my-ah*] called the people together. "Let's rebuild our wall." he said.

"But no one can rebuild that big wall." they complained. "It's impossible!"

"No *one* person, that's true—but all of us working together can." Nehemiah said.

And they did. Merchants and goldsmiths and farmers and seamstresses and priests—none of them had been trained in building huge walls. But working together and praying together, they did it. The girls and women also helped complete this enormous task.

Finally the wall was done. It was so huge there was room for a road on top. Nehemiah decided to celebrate. He called all the people together. The priest Ezra read to them from God's Word. They confessed their sins to God and gave Him offerings. They built little booths of tree branches to live in for a while to remember the years Moses and the people lived in the desert.

Then they had a huge parade on top of the wall. Two choirs with trumpets and other instruments marched—each going opposite directions until they met. The women and little children joined in the singing and celebrated as they watched this parade.

Yes, it had all been hard work. But they did it with God's help. Is there something hard in your life you need God's help for, too?

A Verse to Remember

"Let everything that has breath praise the Lord."

—Psalm 150:6

Planning a Picnic

Summer's a great time for a picnic outdoors. So are the spring and fall, as long as it's not pouring rain. But you can also have indoor picnics all year. You can have just about any food at a picnic, but the best foods are those that are easy to prepare, easy to pack, and easy to eat. You also need to be able to keep perishable foods like ice cream or hot dogs cold or hot so they won't spoil. This is especially true of potato salad. Coolers are good for this.

For a great picnic, first decide how many you expect to attend. Then figure out what you will need as far as paper plates, napkins, plastic forks, and other utensils. Decide whether you're going to precook the meat or grill it when you arrive at your picnic destination (such as a park or the beach). If you plan to have a fire there, make sure it is safely contained in a metal grill or by rocks, with no bushes, twigs, or dry leaves nearby. You'll need charcoal or dry wood and something to start a fire. Always make sure an adult is there to help supervise.

For many people, the word "picnic" means fried chicken (prepared at home or at a restaurant) or hot dogs or hamburgers (grilled when you arrive). For hot dogs and hamburgers, make sure you have enough buns, catsup, mustard, and relish or pickles. You can also be creative with tacos, burritos, pitas, pizza, or other favorite foods. Even PB&Js (peanut butter and jelly) and other sandwiches work well for picnics.

Salads are always great on a hot day. Most people love potato salad, cole slaw, and deviled eggs. Sliced tomatoes and cucumbers are also a fun idea, especially when they are fresh from the garden.

Other good picnic foods are baked beans, potato chips, watermelon, and ice cream (make sure it's packed in plenty of ice). Good desserts are cookies or pie. Top it off with sodas, bottles of water, iced tea, or ice cold lemonade. Mmm! I'm already hungry. Aren't you?

Oh, one more thing—clean up. Ask everyone to help pick up every piece of trash left over, including cans and bottles. If there is no trash container handy, put your trash in a plastic or paper bag and take it home to discard. Keeping God's outdoors beautiful is everyone's job.

Class in a Glass

Everyone loves lemonade in the summertime. That's why kids are always setting up lemonade stands and selling it. Want some lemonade for your picnic? You have at least four choices: bottled, frozen, fresh, or canned.

Bottled: You can purchase 2 liter bottles of lemonade inexpensively. Chill and pour over ice cubes.

Frozen: Buy frozen cartons of lemonade extract (plain or pink) and follow the directions on the carton. Be sure to chill it afterward.

Fresh: Use fresh lemons. Cut in two and squeeze the juice out, getting rid of the seeds. For each cup of water you will need 1 ½ tablespoons of lemon juice and 3 to 4 tablespoons of sugar.
You can just pour the sugar in. Or you can boil the sugar and water for two minutes, until it forms a syrup, and then pour it in. Lemon slices add an eye-appealing "twist."

Canned: Buy aluminum cans of lemonade or lemon-lime drink or soda, chill them, and drink. Whichever "recipe" you use, have a great picnic.

The Greatest Show on Earth Puzzle

Add Secret Letter "E" for "eager to praise God" in space 11 of the puzzle on pg. 27.

Cocky Puts on a Show

Guess who was a star at the barnstorming concert? Connect the dots on the following page to see whose performance was the noisiest at the show.

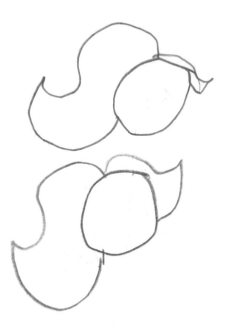

Chapter 3

Down on the Farm

"Le! Guess what?" Sam said when Le finally answered the phone. "I just got a card in the mail from Brittany—you know, from Florida where she's on vacation. Here's what she says:

"'Hi, Sam. My cousin Nicole and I are having a ball at the beach. And I met the coolest lady on the flight down here. Her name's Matty Hawkins. She's a vacationing school teacher from Ohio. But here's what's awesome: She's an exact copy of Miss Kitty! I mean, she even talks just like her. She's a Christian, too, and a great snorkeler. What do you think of that? Tell everyone I miss them and I'll be home soon. But not before I get a perfect tan.'"

Sam sighed. "So how come Brittany's getting all the fun and we're stuck here in Nowheresville?"

"Sam!" Le laughed. "There you go complaining again. What about our backyard pool party and the picnic after our work day and barnstorming concert? Weren't they fun?"

"Yeah, but they're over. And it's not time for the Fair yet. So what are we going to do in between?"

"Well, I know what I'm going to do right now. Take my pup out for a walk. I'm training her to use the leash. We can go down to the Bark Park. Want to ask Sneezit if he'd like to join us? Maria can bring her pup along if she wants to."

Sam laughed. "Sneezit says, 'Meet you at the corner in five minutes.'"

In a few minutes all three girls and pooches reached the Bark Park. The young pups were already bigger than Sneezit and ran circles around him. But he loved it. How beautiful it was out under the trees. Even the butterflies and birds seemed to be having a good time.

Sam told Maria about Brittany's card. "I think I'll e-mail Brittany and ask where this lady is from," Maria said. "Wouldn't it be funny if Matty and Miss Kitty were related somehow?"

Just then Le got a call on her cell phone. It was their old friend, Ric Romero.

"Hey!" he cried excitedly. "Good news, girl! We're doing great out here in Summer City. In fact, Uncle Max has been able to buy us a place of our own—out in the country. Complete with chickens and ducks and a goat and a horse. You'll love the horse. Gallant is gentle as a lamb. And Uncle Max has invited all the Zone 56ers out for a party. How about next Saturday? I sure miss everyone," he added, "so I hope you can come."

The girls could hardly wait. And what a day it was! Lilia Lancaster came along and told Ric all about raising chickens. Ducks were everywhere, waddling and quacking and swimming in a little pond and shaking the water off afterward. Getcha the goat kept everyone amused. Gallant turned out to be great fun, as well as a trick horse. Everyone wanted a ride. "I've already signed him up for the trick riding competition at the County Fair," Ric announced.

Sam stared at him. "County Fair? Already? But isn't that way at the end of the summer?"

Ric laughed and pointed to a poster up on the barn wall. "Nope. It's just three weeks from now— creeping right up on us. So what contests are *you* girls going to enter?"

"My Granny B is going to enter some quilts she made," LaToya said. "And Mom's entering one of her

famous sweet potato pies and some pickles."

"My folks always enter paintings," Sara said.

Sam sighed. "All those dolls we made dresses for would have been perfect for the Fair. But we've already given them away. So what do we have to show now?"

Pastor Andy gave Getcha a good scratching around his horns. "What about something to tell people about Jesus? Something to show God's love to everyone and all He's done for them, including His marvelous creations?"

Ric grinned. "Wow! Now that would be the greatest show on earth! Ideas, anyone?"

Sam nodded. "Yes, what can we do to tell people about Jesus? Something real and true—but something very, very fun?"

· Good News · from God's Word

Why do people like to go camping? Because there's something very exciting being out in nature away from the noise of civilization. What if you lived with Adam and Eve—in a world where there were no towns or cities at all?

Eve's Family Appreciates God's Creations

FROM GENESIS 1:1-4:4

Once, of course, there were no people at all in the world. First there was a world without plants, then God created them. Next He created animals. Then He created people—but just one of them at first. Just one man named Adam.

Adam learned all about each of the animals and gave them all names. He learned about all the plants in the Garden of Eden where he lived, and gave them names, too. He was kind to the animals, and he took care of the trees and other plants. But he was lonely.

How thrilled he was the day God created the very first woman. Now Adam had someone to talk with, someone who could understand him. He told her all about the plants and animals so she could appreciate them too.

Sadly, even though they knew God loved them, and even though they appreciated His creation very much, they didn't always obey Him. So one day God had to send them away from the beautiful garden where they lived and out into the big world.

Life was harder there. They found weeds and rocks and insects that wanted to eat up their crops. But still they were surrounded by God's beautiful world of trees and mountains and valleys and rivers and lakes and seas. As their children were born, Adam and Eve taught them to appreciate God's wonderful world, take care of it, and be thankful to God for it.

We still live in that beautiful world today. We need to take care of it and thank God for it, too.

A Verse to Remember

"He has made everything beautiful in its time."

—Ecclesiastes 3:11

It's a Zoo Out There!

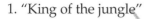

The Bible is full of references to animals. Match as many as you can!

1. "King of the jungle"

2. "Man's best friend"

3. This turns into a butterfly

4. A calf's mother

5. Another name for "rooster"

6. One hump or two?

7. This swims, has fins, and is good to eat

8. An animal like a rabbit

9. They hop and croak

10. Another name for a snake

11. This bird is associated with peace

12. Jesus rode one on Palm Sunday

A. camel (Genesis 24:64)

B. serpent (Genesis 3:1)

C. donkey (Matthew 21:1-4)

D. hare (Leviticus 11:6)

E. dove (Genesis 8:8)

F. lion (Hosea 11:10)

G. frogs (Exodus 8:2)

H. cow (Job 21:10)

I. fish (John 21:10)

J. dog (Judges 7:5)

K. cock (Matthew 26:34)

L. caterpillar (1 Kings 8:37)

The Greatest Show on Earth Puzzle

Add Secret Letter "V" for "valuing all of God's creations" to space 7 of the puzzle on pg. 27.

Abisola

Chapter 4

Greatest Show on Earth

The PTs could hardly wait for Sunday so they could tell Miss Kitty about the County Fair, about Brittany's new friend in Florida, *and* about Ric's new farm.

"He's got the coolest horse I've ever seen." Sara told the class. "His name's Gallant, and he loves to eat apples out of your hand. I can't wait for my big brother Tony to meet him."

"You should see his tricks." LaToya added. "Ric's going to enter him in the County Fair. I bet he wins."

"Miss Kitty," Sam said, "Pastor Andy said that instead of entering something ourselves so that we could show off, maybe we should show off Jesus instead. You know, show God's love to everyone. How can we do that?"

"Hmm," their teacher answered. "Well, you remember how they have all those booths at the Fair—for taking pictures and selling popcorn and everything? What if we rent one and call it a 'Youth Booth' for kids and teens? We could have fliers and tell Bible stories."

Maria grinned. "And do chalk talks and put on little puppet shows, all for free. We could even give away lemonade."

Sam rolled her eyes. "There's that 'lemonade' thing again. Don't people ever get tired of drinking it?"

"Not when they're hot and thirsty," Jenna retorted. "It's cheap, easy to fix, and great for vitamin C. We could even give away frozen lemon pops. We could call them Lemon Licks."

Miss Kitty nodded and smiled. "Those are all great ideas. I'll look into renting a booth right way.

And I'll call Pastor Andy and Pastor McConahan to see if they have some ideas, too."

After they read the story in their Bibles of the Samaritan woman who shared the Good News about Jesus with her friends, Le said, "That's just what we could be doing at the Fair. Sharing the best news on earth!"

"Oh, speaking of good news," Sam added, "Miss Kitty, Brittany wrote and said she met someone on her flight down to Florida who looks and talks exactly like you. Just about your age. She's a Christian, too. Brittany and Nicole think she's great. The main difference is that she can snorkel and you can't."

Everyone laughed at that. "Well, not yet I can't," Miss Kitty admitted, "but that doesn't mean I couldn't if I tried. What's this lady's name?"

"Matty. Matty Hawkins."

Their teacher frowned. "Now isn't that interesting? I used to know a little girl named Matty when I was young. I think she was with me in an orphanage down in Mississippi before I was sent to the one in Tennessee—you know, the one Ma Jones directed. People used to call us the Twinkle Twins because we looked so much alike."

As everyone was leaving, Miss Kitty said, "Your assignment for the week is to think of as many ways as possible to turn our Youth Booth into 'The Greatest Show on Earth.'"

"And," Sam whispered to Maria, "to look on the Internet and see what we can find out about this Matty person, right?"

Maria high-fived Sam. "Right, Sherlock. The plot thickens!"

· Good News · from God's Word

Sam and her friends tried to think of ways to share the Gospel with the visitors at the Fair. In this story, Jesus shared the Gospel with an unbeliever—through a drink of water.

Sharing the Good News

JOHN 4:1-4

Did you ever grumble about hot summer days? One lady back in Jesus' time really had something to grumble about. She lived in the land of Samaria in a small town called Sychar [sigh-car]. Each day she had to walk a long distance from home carrying an empty clay jug. Then when she filled it, she would have to carry it back home. It would be even heavier then. Bummer, right?

Nobody had faucets with running water back then. And all the other women of her city had to get their water in the exact same way. But they would go first thing in the morning when it was cool. She used to go in the morning, too, but the other women made fun of her and called her names because she had been married several times. Getting tired of this treament, she went in the heat of the day so no one would be around to torment her.

But one day when she came to the well, someone was already sitting there—Jesus. He was resting while His friends went into town to buy them all some lunch. Jesus smiled at her. "Could you please give me a drink of water?" He asked.

She stared at Him. Right off, she could tell He was a Jew by the way He was dressed. "You're not supposed to ask me for a drink," she protested. You see, in those days the Jews thought they were better than the people of Samaria. That wasn't very nice of them, was it?

Then Jesus told her about the living water of the Gospel, and how believing in Him would give her everlasting life. She was so amazed and excited that she put down her jug and ran right back to town. She told everyone she saw, "Hey, you! Come out to the well! The Messiah is there!"

So the woman Jesus had shared the Gospel with then shared it with everyone in town—and they rushed out to the well to hear it for themselves. Many of them became believers, all because Jesus shared the Gospel.

A Verse to Remember

"You will receive power when the Holy Spirit comes on you; and you will be my witnesses."

–Acts 1:8

How to Share the Gospel

Want to help others know more about Jesus? Simply cross out the numbers from each sentence and then divide the remaining letters into separate words.

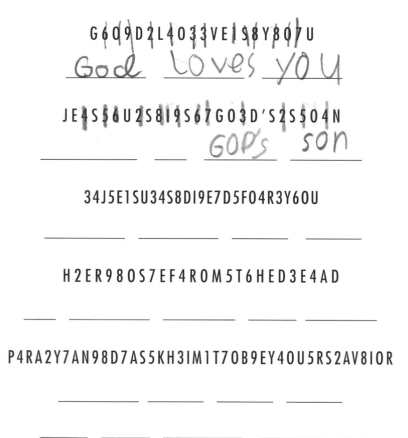

G6Q9D2L4O3̶3VE̶I̶S8Y8O̶7U

God̲ L̲oves̲ yo̲u̲

JE4̶S5̶6U2̶S8I̶9S6̶7GO3̶D'S2̶S5O4N

GOD's̲ son̲

34J5E1SU34S8DI9E7D5FO4R3Y6OU

_____ _____ ____ ____

H2ER98OS7EF4ROM5T6HED3E4AD

___ ____ _____ ____

P4RA2Y7AN98D7AS5KH3IM1T7OB9EY4OU5RS2AV8IOR

_____ ____ ___ _____ _____

_____ ____ ____ _____

The Greatest Show on Earth Puzzle

Add Secret Letter "G" for "Gospel-sharing" in space 1 of the puzzle on pg. 27.

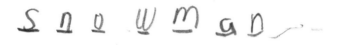

Chapter 5

Christmas in July

What a week that was. The PTs zoomed
around like a whirlwind trying to figure out which
Bible story to use for their daily hand-puppet show.
Finally they decided on Christmas—yes, the story of
the very first Christmas. In the middle of the summer!
The decided to call their show "Christmas in July."

Sara's parents, who were artists, taught them how to make papier-mâché [*pay-per muh-shay*] heads  for their characters out of paper strips, water, and paste. They had to mold each one, let it dry, and paint it. There were so many puppets to make. Donkeys and sheep and shepherds and Wise Men. The PTs even made a big papier-mâché star.

Some puppets were little marionettes, moved by strings or sticks. But most were hand puppets, moved with the girls' fingers.

Lilia and Angie did all the faces. Granny B and Jenna's mom helped make the little puppet bodies and costumes with room to put hands and fingers through to move the puppets.

By now Sonya was back from vacation. She and Sara wrote a script for the puppet play, while Sara's big brother Tony and their friends Ryan and Kevin helped make a little puppet theater to use at their Youth Booth. They painted some little backdrops, too, for the shepherds out in the field and the manger scene in town.

Meanwhile, Miss Kitty was able to rent a booth at the Fair. They decided to keep it open from 1-4 p.m. each of the three days of the Fair. They would have Gospel tracts and flyers about their church available for people to pick up even when the PTs weren't there.

Everyone pitched in to help paint posters and big banners to put up on their booth. Maria used her computer to make free tickets for their shows to hand out to children.

She was using her computer for something else, too: trying to discover anything she could about Miss Kitty's early years at the orphanages in Mississippi and Tennessee and any information about someone named Matty Hawkins. But she didn't find anything.

Then when she checked her email, she saw a note from Brittany.

"Hi, Maria!" Brittany wrote. "Thought you PTs would enjoy seeing these pictures of me and Nicole on the beach. That's Miss Matty in the snorkeling outfit. And she also had a picture in her wallet she let me see, about when she was a little girl—a picture  of her and her best friend. So I've included that, too."

Maria could hardly wait to download the pictures. The beach one was funny. But the other one really caught her eye. It was of two little girls, almost identical, both with coal-black hair and big smiles. And it was signed "Matty and Kitty"!

What was the mystery of the "Twinkle Twins"?

· Good News ·
from God's Word

We all love mysteries, don't we? Mysteries like why God chose David when he was just a young teenager. But as David became older, people began to understand. See if you can too!

Songs of Praise for David
1 SAMUEL 17:2-18:7

When David was just a young teenager, God chose Him to be King Saul's successor. But of course David didn't become King right away. He kept right on with his chores—taking care of the family sheep. That's where he learned to be brave and fight off lions and wolves and bears that wanted to eat his sheep.

That's also where he had time to sit and make up songs and sing them. Eventually he wrote magnificent hymns that are recorded for us in the Book of Psalms.

Now Saul, who was King of Israel at the time, was a very unhappy man. He was unhappy because he was angry at God and refused to tell God he was sorry for what he did wrong. So he would sit and mope and pout and not want to talk to anyone.

This worried his servants. So they started a nation-wide search for someone who was a good musician to come to the King's palace. They wanted someone to play beautiful music for the King so he would feel better—like a big talent contest. Well, they didn't have to search for long. Young David fit the bill perfectly.

Whenever King Saul was feeling down, he would send for David. David would come, play for him, help him feel better, then go back home.

But King Saul had other problems too. The giant Goliath appeared with the Philistine army. "Come fight me!" he would taunt the Jews. Goliath was so big—over nine feet tall—that everyone was afraid of him. Even King Saul was afraid.

"I'll fight him,"
David volunteered.
And he did. A
young boy with
just a slingshot
brought down a
nine-foot giant
covered with
armor. He could do
this because God was
with him.

When people heard the
news about David's victory, he became a national
hero. Women and girls came out from all the towns
of Israel to meet King Saul and David. They sang and
danced and played tambourines and lutes. But they
praised David more than the King.

The people were thrilled that young David
trusted in God and destroyed the giant!

A Verse to Remember

*"Never be lacking in zeal, but keep your
spiritual fervor, serving the Lord."*
–Romans 12:11

Searching for David!
A Word Search Puzzle

From the list below, see how many of the capitalized words telling about David you can find in the puzzle. Remember, words can go right to left or left to right, also from bottom to top and from top to bottom.

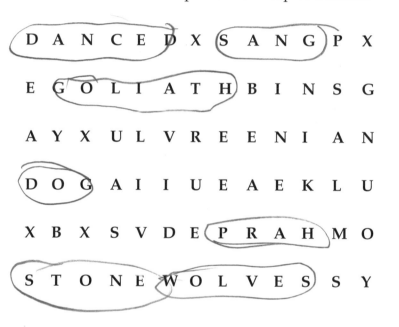

```
D  A  N  C  E  D  X  S  A  N  G  P  X
E  G  O  L  I  A  T  H  B  I  N  S  G
A  Y  X  U  L  V  R  E  E  N  I  A  N
D  O  G  A  I  I  U  E  A  E  K  L  U
X  B  X  S  V  D  E  P  R  A  H  M  O
S  T  O  N  E  W  O  L  V  E  S  S  Y
```

Horizontal search words (going both left and right)

- David played on a small HARP
- David SANG for King Saul
- GOD was with David
- The girls and women DANCED for joy
- David used a STONE in his slingshot
- WOLVES tried to kill David's sheep
- GOLIATH was a giant

63

Vertical (going both up and down)

- David was young, still a BOY
- He watched his family's SHEEP
- The King's name was SAUL
- David wanted to LIVE for God
- One little stone and Goliath was DEAD
- He was still quite YOUNG
- The shepherd boy's name was DAVID
- He wanted to be TRUE to God
- Sometimes he had to fight a BEAR
- Goliath was NINE feet tall
- David wrote the Book of PSALMS

The Greatest Show on Earth Puzzle

Add Secret Letter "E" for "energetic for God" in space 8 of the puzzle on pg. 27.

Chapter 6

Stung by a Beetle

Plans for the fair were going great—
absolutely perfect. The stage was all built, the
backdrops painted, the stage curtains in place,

all the puppets made, painted, and dressed. Both the Zone 56 kids and the High School group (God's HI Way) were involved. Even Sara's big brother Tony helped when he wasn't at his job flipping burgers at the Yum-Yum Palace.

"'Way to go!" Pastor Andy complimented everyone. They had set the stage up in LaToya's yard, under some big shady trees. They also had picnic tables and folding chairs out there to practice music for their show. Instead of "Toot 'n Granny," this time their group called themselves "The Rubber Band." Cocky, Rocky, and Pooch from the McAfee Farm and Sneezit would all be part of it. They even had an old wash tub, and some giant rubber bands for "harps."

LaToya told her neighbors what they would be doing for the next couple of hours, so they wouldn't think a huge thunderstorm had arrived. Then soon everyone was jamming. LaToya thought she had never had such fun.

Suddenly they heard, "Boy, that stinks!"

Looking around, LaToya saw four guys peering over the top of her fence. "Quit disturbing the peace, you losers," one shouted. "Learn how to play before you make the rest of us listen to this noise," said another. LaToya's heart sank. It was Beetle Boxer and his three pals.

"We're practicing for the Fair," she told them.

"Not any more," Beetle replied. And suddenly he sprayed them all over with a huge squirt gun. "So long, suckers," he yelled as he and his friends sped off on their bikes.

After they left, the PTs and their friends surveyed the damage. Granny B brought out a hair dryer to dry the stage curtains and puppets. But some of them and one backdrop would have to be repainted. After they finished the repair work, they took everything over to Sam's back patio and threw tarps over it all. Maybe it would be safer there.

But the next morning, disaster! Someone had climbed over the Pearsons' back fence, pulled off the tarps, and sprayed red paint over everything. They'd even sprayed "Losers!" on the fence.

"That does it!" Sam cried. "No more being the nice guy!"

"Right," sobbed little Petie. "I betcha Beetle and his jerk friends did it. Let's go find them and beat them up."

But when Miss Kitty heard about it, she replied, "Remember, the Bible says we should reward evil with good."

So finally everyone decided to make two big banners. They put one out front of LaToya's home, and one out front of Sam's. The banners both said, "We forgive you. God forgives you, too," along with cartoons of bright red beetles.

Would Beetle see them? If so, what would he do?

· Good News ·
from God's Word

Sam's friends want to act the right way toward
Beetle. But knowing which is the best way to act can be
hard. King Solomon was faced with that decision, too—
how best to help a baby in need.

King Solomon Helps a Baby

1 Kings 3:16-28

When Solomon became King, he asked God to
make him wise so he could make good decisions.
And God promised that He would.

Soon afterward, two very sad women came to
see Solomon, bringing one tiny baby with them.
Today such women would go to the police for help.
But in those days they could go directly to the King.
"What's the matter?" King Solomon asked.

They explained that they both lived in the
same house, and they both had just had babies. But
one of the babies had died. "So that other woman
took my baby to replace her dead baby!" sobbed one
of the mothers.

"No, she's lying!" cried the other one. "This
baby is mine! Hers was the dead one!"

They didn't have DNA testing in those days,
so King Solomon couldn't prove scientifically which
woman the living baby belonged to. Instead, he

used wisdom. "Well," he said, "since there are two of you women and just one baby, I guess to be fair we'll have to cut the baby in two and give you each a half."

One shrugged. "Fine with me," she said.

"Oh, no," cried the other one. "Don't hurt the poor little baby. I'd rather you give it to that other woman than have anything bad happen to it."

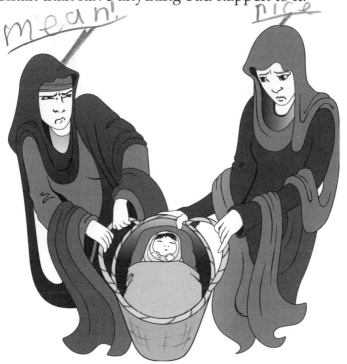

King Solomon nodded. "I see that *you* are the real mother with real love for your child," he said. "So the baby is yours. Take it home and love it."

How glad the real mother was to hold her little one in her arms again. And how thankful she was for the King's wise decision.

A Verse to Remember

"Do not be overcome by evil, but overcome evil with good."

–Romans 12:21

Sing Along

Here are some of the silly songs the "Rubber Band" was practicing for the Fair. Maybe you and your friends would like to sing them, too.

Some silly verses for **"Old MacDonald Had a Farm"**

Old MacDonald had a horse, E-I-E-I-O,
He "nagged" that horse to death, of course, E-I-E-I-O.
With a giddyup here and a giddyup there,
Giddyup, giddyup everywhere.
Old MacDonald had a horse, E-I-E-I-O.

Old MacDonald had a cow, E-I-E-I-O,
He needed to milk her but he didn't know how,
E-I-E-I-O.
With a "moo-moo" here
and a "moo-moo" there,
And a "stop, you dumb
cow" everywhere.
Old MacDonald had a
cow, E-I-E-I-O.

Old MacDonald had a pig, E-I-E-I-O,
But that pig was just too big, E-I-E-I-O.
He ate up the corn and he ate up the barn
And soon ate everything on the farm!
Old MacDonald had a pig, E-I-E-I-O.

And for **"I've Been Working on the Railroad"**
I've been working in the barnyard
All the livelong day.
I've been working in the barnyard
Just to pass the time away.
Can't you hear the whistle blowing,
"Rise up so early in the morn?"
Can't you hear the farmer yelling,
"Get out and hoe that corn!"

Farmhand, won't you hoe,
Farmhand, won't you hoe,
Farmhand, won't you hoe that corn?
[repeat those 3 lines]

The Greatest Show on Earth Puzzle

Add Secret Letter "R" for "repaying good with evil" to space 14 of the puzzle on pg. 27.

Chapter 7

Can't Beat 'Em?
Join 'Em!

Finally everything was patched up, repainted, and once more ready to use. "Such a waste of time," Sonya sighed. "Why are there bad people in the world, anyway?"

"We were cramped for time already," Sara complained. "It's just not fair."

73

Pastor Andy gave her a pat on the back. "Cheer up, kid. Your band is fantastic. Let's give the play and all the songs another try, then run down to the Yum-Yum Palace for burgers and fries for everyone. I'll buy."

So everyone got back into the swing of things. And then—

"Well, if it isn't you losers again." Beetle and his gang were back, peering over Sam's fence. "You guys just don't know when to give up, do you?"

Pastor Andy walked over to them. "Not when we're doing something for God. God's guys and girls never give up. So how about you stop your lame trash-talking and join us instead? Beetle, I hear you play a mean bass."

"Uh, well, yeah, man. Uh, maybe."

"And your buddies—don't they play the drums and trumpet?"

Beetle looked confused. "Yeah, how did you know? I mean, what's it to you, preacher-man?"

"Well, I'm giving you all an offer. Run home and get your instruments right now and jam with us. Or, we can take that bit about the red paint straight to the police. What do you say? And after our practice, everyone gets burgers and fries at Yum-Yum."

"Oh, man," Beetle cried. "That fine double-burger 'Monster Mouthful' combo?"

"You got it," Sara laughed. "Grilled by my own brother."

So five minutes later the band had four new members. "You guys are good," Beetle finally admitted.

"So are you," Le replied. "Now let's see how good you are at eating the Monster Mouthful."

At the restaurant, Beetle turned bright red when Pastor Andy led them all in thanking God for their food. But soon he and his pals relaxed and started talking with everyone.

Finally Beetle said, "Look, guys, I'm sorry we screwed up and hurt your stuff. Is there any way we can make it up to you?"

"Come join us at the Fair," Sara said, "at the Youth Booth and the concert stage. We're going to have fun and give fun. And best of all, we'll tell folks about God."

"We'd love to have you," Miss Kitty added.

 Suddenly Maria jumped up. "Miss Kitty," she said. "I forgot to show you something. Something I think you'll really like."

And she pulled out the pictures Brittany had sent her. Her teacher took one look—and her eyes widened!

· Good News ·
from God's Word

Yes, Beetle finally admitted he was wrong and tried to do better. But not everyone will change their ways—including the woman in this Bible story.

An Unkind Woman's Demand
MATTHEW 14:1-12

Not everyone in the world is good and kind. Not all men and boys. And not all women and girls. This is because Satan tries to tempt everyone to do wrong things. Some people grow up around so much sin they don't even recognize right from wrong. Some just don't care, either.

One of the wicked women in Jesus' time was named Herodias [hair-oh-dee-us]. She had married a ruler, Herod Philip, her uncle. Then she left him to live with another uncle, her husband's brother, Herod Antipas [hair-ud an-tih-pus].

This of course was forbidden in the Mosaic law, and John the Baptist had warned her about it. But Herodias didn't care. She was very beautiful and very ambitious. She wanted what she wanted and she would do anything to get it—including getting rid of John the Baptist. How dare he tell her she was sinning!

That's the way she taught her daughter Salome [sol-uh-may] to live, too.

Salome was a young teenager and very beautiful. She had been studying dance and loved to perform. So when Herod Antipas' birthday came, he threw a huge party for all his friends. Salome danced for everyone.

"Wonderful!" Herod cried. "What can I give you to show my appreciation?"

Salome wasn't sure what to ask, so she checked with her mother. This was the moment her mother had been waiting for. "Ask for the head of John the Baptist on a platter," Herodias said.

So Salome did. Herod didn't want to go back

on his word. So, a great man of God lost his life all because an unkind woman wanted to have her way regardless of the price.

But John the Baptist went straight to heaven to be forever with God, while Herodias only sank deeper and deeper into sin. Disobeying God's Word is never the way to win. Those who obey God are always winners.

A Verse to Remember

"You are the light of the world."

–Matthew 5:14

The Greatest Show on Earth Puzzle

Add Secret Letter "E" for "even-handed response" in space 18 of the puzzle on pg. 27.

Ready for the Puppet Show

Imagine that the scene on the following page is the stage the PTs and their friends made for the puppet show. Draw a Christmas manger scene like the one that the PTs were going to show with their puppets.

Chapter 8

Pix, Puppets, and Pools

At first Miss Kitty couldn't see the pictures Maria had handed her very well. "They're kind of blurry," she decided, "especially this one of the two little girls. And they've been printed from the computer using a black and white printer, so—"

Then she took a closer look at the beach scene. "Hey, Brittany's getting a real tan, isn't she? And that must be the lady snorkeler she's been talking about. This other picture with the little girls must have been taken about 15 or 20 years ago, judging by the way the kids are dressed. And there's some writing on it. It says—"

Suddenly her face went white. If Pastor Andy hadn't caught her, she might have collapsed completely. He sat her down while LaToya poured some bottled water on a handkerchief, wrung it out, and pressed it against her face. Finally she could speak. "I-It's signed, 'Matty and Kitty,'" she whispered. "Th-That's me, and that other little girl—well, I-I think she's from the orphanage in Mississippi. Y-Yes, I t-told you we were called the Twinkle Twins. I should remember more, but I can't. I don't know why."

Maria frowned. "Well, don't you worry, Miss Kitty. We'll get to the bottom of this. Maybe this new friend of Brittany's knows the answer. Or maybe Ma Jones does." Suddenly she grinned. "Oh, I love good mysteries! I get to play detective!"

"Meanwhile," Pastor Andy said, "I'm going to get Miss Kitty home. I think part of her problem is that she's overheated. Maybe all of us are, we've been working so hard. So what do you say tomorrow after practice we all head over to the Circleville City Pool and cool off?"

That evening Maria went back on her computer. *Brittany,* she wrote, *I know you're coming home soon. But would you please ask your friend Miss Matty what she knows about that picture of her and the other little girl? When Miss Kitty saw it, she was so shocked she almost passed out. Maybe Miss Matty can help us find out more about Miss Kitty's family. And by the way, hurry home. Our new "Rubber Band" and the puppet show aren't complete without you. Maybe Miss Matty could come visit us, too. TTUL, Maria*

After practice the next day, everyone grabbed their towels and sunscreen and started walking together down to the pool. On the way they passed by Shawnee Park. "Look," Ryan said. "Isn't that Beetle and his friends?"

It sure was. They had used scrap lumber to make skateboard ramps. They were also skateboarding down the metal stair rails by the bandstand, all without helmets.

"Hey, man," Pastor Andy called. "You guys are good. But you need helmets. And you need a real skate park—like the one over in Summer City."

"I like to skate that one," Sara said. "You can really do leaps and jumps there."

Beetle stared at her. "Girls? On skateboards?"

"I'd be glad to take you there sometime,"

Pastor Andy said. "Sorry you missed practice today. Right now we're headed for the pool. Want to come along?"

"Yes, sir." Everyone helped Beetle and his friends pick up their pieces of lumber. Then they all headed down to the pool. Sam was amazed how Beetle changed when he was just relaxing and having a good time. "We're going to practice again tomorrow for the Fair," she said. "Why don't you come join us then?"

Beetle shrugged. "Well, maybe. You know, I used to go to church once myself. But no matter how much I tried to do what the pastor said, he told me I was just going to hell. So I gave up."

"Well, God hasn't given up on you," Kevin told him. "Come back tomorrow and see!"

Sam held her breath. Would Beetle really come?

· Good News ·
from God's Word

Some people, like Beetle, think they can never be good enough for God, so why bother? But of course none of us are good enough. That's why God sent His Son Jesus and invites everyone to join His family. Another name for that family is the church.

Christ's Bride, the Church
REVELATION 19:6-9

Everyone loves a wedding! It's all so romantic! People are all so happy that the bride and groom have found and fallen in love with each other.

We want to see what kind of wedding gown the bride will wear, and how she will arrange her hair. Everyone cries when the bride and groom say, "I do," and then kiss. At that point we want to say, "And they both lived happily ever after."

Of course, not all marriages "live happily ever after." Problems arise with finances, health, stress, personality differences. Children bring joy, but also new responsibilities.

But there is one wedding where the Bride and

the Groom will both really live happily ever after. And so will everyone there. It's about a wonderful celebration that will happen at the end of time. For the Groom is none other than Jesus. And the Bride is His Church. You see, Jesus loves all Christians so much He wants to bring us into His heavenly home to be with Him forever—just as a groom in this world goes with his new bride to their own new home.

What a great day that will be! All believers in God from the beginning of time will be there, singing and celebrating. So will the angels. And so will God Himself.

And so will you if you have given your heart to Jesus. If you haven't, why not do so today? Turn to "Do You Have Two Birthdays" in the "Extra Stuff" section of this book. There you'll learn how you too can become a child of God and be with Him forever.

A Verse to Remember

"Always be prepared to give an answer to everyone who asks you to give the reason for the hope that you have."

—1 Peter 3:15

The Greatest Show on Earth Puzzle

Add Secret Letter "D" for "daring to tell about Christ" in space 3 of the puzzle on pg. 27.

The A-Maze-ing Skate Park!

Sara loves to ride her skateboard in the maze at the Skate Park. See if you can help her find the fastest way through the maze from the entrance to the exit.

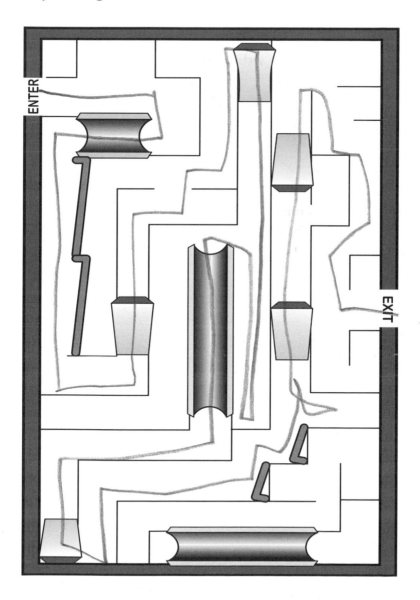

Chapter 9

This Fair's Not Fair!

The minute Brittany got home from her vacation she called Sam. "I'm back!" she cried. "You guys have no idea how much I missed you. Now, what did I hear about puppets and a 'Rubber Band'?"

Sam laughed. "Whoa! I've got questions too. What about this Miss Matty person? Did you find out any more about her?"

"Absolutely. I think she's related to Miss Kitty. I gave her Miss Kitty's phone number. She's going to call Miss Kitty this afternoon so they can see if they can figure things out. Isn't that great? Okay, I haven't unpacked yet. But when's the next practice for the Fair? I'm dying to be there. And wait till you see my great tan and all the neat things Nicole and I found on our shopping trips."

Just then Sam heard some voices in her back yard. "Welcome back, girlfriend," she said quickly. "Don't forget practice this afternoon. Gotta go now and see what all that noise is about."

But when she ran to the back door, she was so surprised she could hardly talk. Beetle and his friends were there— painting the Pearsons' fence, weeding their flowers, and mowing the grass.

"It's the least we could do," Beetle explained, looking rather ashamed. "We want to apologize and make it up to everyone. We did something real stupid. We'd rather do the kind of stuff you guys do. You have fun and love God at the same time."

Sam was amazed and couldn't say a word, but her little brother Petie jumped right in. "You guys can too," he said. "Can't they, Sam?"

Then she found her smile and her voice. "Sure. When you finish up here, let Petie know, and he'll get some sodas and snacks for everyone."

Wow! God was really working on Beetle and his friends. How cool! Sam should be happy, but she was so angry about Brittany's call. It just wasn't fair! Here the rest of them had been working nonstop trying to pull the Youth Booth together for the Fair, while Brittany was off in Florida having the time of her life.

Now that she's back, she wants to be included, just as if she'd been working on the Fair show all the time like the rest of them. It wasn't fair.

When Brittany came by for practice that afternoon, Sam was even more resentful. Brittany was showing off her pictures of Florida and Nicole and Miss Matty. The photos were on her *new* camera phone and her *new* digital camera. She even had a *new* iPod. Sam couldn't afford anything except a little disposable camera. It just wasn't fair.

To make matters worse, Sam then learned that Sonya was going to have a guest soon—a new friend she met on her vacation at the Cherokee Nation, named Little Red Wing. Sam didn't get to go anywhere for her vacation. She had to stay here in lousy old Loserville. It really wasn't fair.

Sam did her best to pull herself together since practice started soon. When Miss Kitty arrived, she was grinning from ear to ear. "Well, kids," she exclaimed to everyone. "Do I have a surprise! Wait till you hear this."

· Good News · from God's Word

There will always be people who have things that we don't—and it's easy to be resentful like Sam. Soon she realized what was really important. So did the woman in our next Bible story.

Mary Magdalene Weeps for Her Lord
JOHN 20:10-18

On the very first Easter morning, Mary Magdalene and a few other women came to the tomb where Jesus was buried. They brought sweet-smelling spices with them to sprinkle over His body to show their love.

We're not sure if the women all arrived at the tomb at the same time, or if they came individually or in groups. But Mary arrived while it was still dark. When she saw that the huge stone had been rolled away from Jesus' tomb, she was amazed. She ran all the way back to town to tell Peter and John. "Come quickly," she cried. "The tomb is empty! I don't know where Jesus is."

So Peter and John ran back to the cemetery with her. They looked in the tomb, too. Mary was right. It was empty. But what could they do? Sadly they returned home.

But Mary stayed right there crying. But suddenly she saw something: two angels in the empty tomb, sitting where Jesus' body had been. "Why are you crying?" they asked her.

"I don't know where Jesus is," she sobbed.

Still sobbing, she turned around and saw someone else there. "Why are you crying? He asked.

"Please, Sir," she sobbed, "just tell me where Jesus is."

Then a voice said, "Mary." It was Jesus' voice. He was the One standing right beside her.

Oh, how thrilled Mary was to know that she didn't have to be sad anymore. And this time when she ran to tell the disciples about it, she didn't have sad news. She had the happiest news in the world! Jesus was alive!

A Verse to Remember

"Love is patient, love is kind. It does not envy, it does not boast, it is not proud."

–1 Corinthians 13:4

When Your Eyes Turn Green

Have you ever been jealous of someone—even a good friend? Jealousy makes you miserable, and makes them miserable, too. Ask God to help you be glad for all He's done for you. And pray that you can show love to the person you've been jealous of.

The Greatest Show on Earth Puzzle

Add Secret Letter "N" for "not resentful" to space 17 of the puzzle on pg. 27.

Who's Who

It's time to see if you remember who's who among the PTs and their friends. Try matching the names with their descriptions.

1. Brittany Boorsma

2. Lilia Lancaster

3. Sonya Silverhorse

4. Petie Pearson

5. Miss Kitty

6. Sara Fields

7. Sneezit

8. Granny B

9. Tony Fields

10. Pastor Andy

11. Angie Andrews

12. Le Tran

13. Maria Moreno

14. Jenna Jenkins

15. Ma Jones

A. once knew a little girl named Matty

B. likes the Skate Park

C. flips burgers at Yum-Yum Palace

D. her father was wounded in the Army

E. helped raise Miss Kitty

F. has a pet rooster, Cocky

G. has twin baby sisters

H. plays the violin (and "fiddle")

I. has a new friend, Little Red Wing

J. has twin brothers, Juan and Ricardo

K. Sam's little brother

L. LaToya's grandmother

M. leads the Zone 56 youth group

N. likes the Bark Park

O. vacationed in Florida

Chapter 10

What's a Twinkle Twin?

"Oh, Miss Kitty. You've got to tell us quick before we explode!" Le begged.

"It's about Matty, isn't it?" Brittany asked.

"You knew her when she was a little girl, didn't you?" Sam added.

"Hey, everyone cool it," Kevin urged. "Let *her* tell it—not *you*."

Miss Kitty sat down on a lawn chair. "I did get to talk to Brittany's new friend," she began. "And we did indeed both live together in that orphanage down in Sweet Water, Missisippi. And people did indeed call us the Twinkle Twins, because we looked so much alike. Then she was adopted by a family in Georgia, and I was transferred to the orphanage in Tennessee. So that's the last we'd heard of each other."

"Until now," Sara said.

Miss Kitty grinned. "Yes, until now. She's unmarried—just like me—and she loves sports and teaching. And we're going to get together next week. She's going to come to the Fair. I'm going to introduce her to Ma Jones, too."

Pastor Andy's eyes twinkled. "Brittany says she looks and talks just like you. I don't know if we can take two of you, can we, gang?"

Sonya gave her a big hug. "I'd love to have ten of you, Miss Kitty."

That way, she thought to herself, *maybe one of you could be my mother.*

In a few minutes Beetle and his pals—all cleaned

up—showed up with their instruments and practiced, too. Then for a treat Pastor Andy took everyone to the Skate Park over in Summer City. Miss Kitty helped drive.

Beetle couldn't wait to show off, so he bet Sara she wouldn't have the nerve to try his skateboarding tricks. He was shocked to discover she already knew them. Not only that, but she was almost better than he was.

That evening when Jenna was telling her mother about the day, she added, "We're planning to serve lemonade and cookies at our Youth Booth. But that sounds kind of lame. Can you think of something else we could serve that wouldn't cost much?"

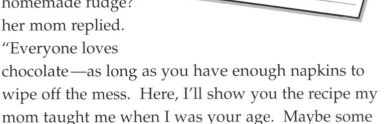

"Why not homemade fudge?" her mom replied. "Everyone loves chocolate—as long as you have enough napkins to wipe off the mess. Here, I'll show you the recipe my mom taught me when I was your age. Maybe some of the other PTs would like to make some too."

Jenna laughed. "And I can think of some guys who would love to sample it...just to make sure it's okay, of course. Including Beetle Boxer."

Get real! How was she going to keep the Zone 56 guys from eating it all before they got to the Fair?

· Good News ·
from God's Word

Jenna was glad that all the Zone 56 gang was working together without any of them bossing the others. That's the Christian way—something Jesus taught the woman in our next Bible story.

A Mother's Request for Her Sons
MATTHEW 20:20-28

The mother of James and John was so proud of her sons. They were good fishermen just like her husband Zebedee [zeh-buh-dee]. They were also two

of Jesus' disciples, traveling with Him to tell people about God. No mother, she was sure, had finer sons than hers.

Then one day she got an idea. Since her sons were such good helpers of Jesus, maybe He should promote them. Maybe they should be Jesus' vice presidents.

So one day she convinced them to go with her to Jesus, to talk about her idea.

"Jesus," she said, "I have a great idea. You don't have any vice presidents. All Your disciples are on the same level. Why don't You have my two sons to be directly under You with one on Your right side and one on Your left? Then they would be over the other disciples and You wouldn't have so much work to do."

But Jesus said, "I'm not the One who promotes people; that is God's place." Then He told all His disciples, "You know that most people in the world want positions of power and authority over other people. But Christians are to be different. You should want to help people instead, just as God sent Me to help you."

 A Verse to Remember

"We have different gifts, according to the grace given us."

–Romans 12:6

Really Truly Fudge

Here's a special recipe for fudge. Make it with adult permission and supervision. Times shown are approximates.

- 2 one-ounce squares unsweetened chocolate (OR ⅓ cup cocoa)
- ¾ cup milk
- 2 cups sugar
- 1 teaspoon light corn syrup
- 2 tablespoons butter or margarine (OR 3 tablespoons if using cocoa)
- 1 teaspoon vanilla
- Total preparation time: 50-60 minutes

Melt the chocolate (or cocoa) by heating it with the milk in a saucepan on medium-low heat (5 minutes). Add sugar and corn syrup, stirring until the sugar dissolves (2 minutes). While stirring frequently, continue cooking on med-low heat until a drop of your fudge mixture forms a tiny ball that stays together when dropped into a cup of very cold water (15-20 minutes). Remove from heat, add butter, and cool at room temperature to lukewarm without stirring (20 minutes). Add the vanilla and beat rigorously until fudge becomes very thick (5-10 minutes). Immediately spread in a greased pan. When firm, cut into squares.

The Greatest Show on Earth Puzzle

Add Secret Letter "L" for "learning to appreciate each other" to space 5 of the puzzle on pg. 27.

Chapter 11

Bridesmaids–and Broke

The next morning the PTs got together for a fudge-making party. Even Miss Kitty took the morning off from work to help.

"Whew!" Sam exclaimed. "We're all making fudge and music and plans for the Fair. Not exactly what I'd call a relaxing summer."

"Yeah," Le sighed. "And that's not all. Mom and her fiancé are busy making plans for their upcoming wedding. Between that and the Fair, my head's spinning. I mean, I'm still getting used to calling Dr. Phan 'Poppa.' And having two new little brothers. And moving to a new home where there's room for us."

"Plus all the PTs have been invited to be bridesmaids," Sam replied. "I think that's great. But that means getting fitted for dresses—right here in the middle of the hottest summer on record."

"Are Dr. Phan's little boys going to dress up, too?" Maria asked.

"Uh-huh. Would you believe that Mom's renting little tuxedos for both of them?"

Sara stirred her pot of fudge. "So who's going to stay with you and Dr. Phan's boys while your folks are on their honeymoon?"

Le shrugged. "I dunno. Neither Mom nor Poppa Phan have living parents. So it's not like our grandparents can come stay with us."

Sam grinned. "Then I guess you'll just have to go along on the honeymoon!"

Le tried to smile, but it didn't work. "Miss Kitty," she sighed, "why is life so complicated? Why do people have to fall in love and get married?"

"Because God wants us to have happy homes," their teacher replied. "Even though my parents died when I was very small, I'm glad they loved each other, and loved me, too."

"I know," Sonya said. "Dad and I are talking about adopting Little Red Wing to be my sister. It would be hard having a new sister. But still, I love the idea of having a sister to giggle with and share clothes with and stuff."

Sam thought for a minute. "I don't think Beetle Boxer has a happy home. He seems unhappy, just like Ric Romero was before he came to know Jesus. I think I'm going to add Beetle to my prayer list."

Just then the mail arrived. "Look!" Sam cried. "Flyers about the Fair. Wow, I can hardly wait. Ferris wheels and cotton candy and rodeo riding and hot dogs and everything! LaToya— check this out."

"I'm checking, all right," she replied. "I'm looking at the price to get in: $5 each plus the cost for the rides and all the rest. I don't know about you, but I'm broke."

The PTs stared at each other. "Oh, no!" Sam moaned. "We forgot about tickets, and we're all broke, too. Now how are we going to get into the Fair? Or have any fun when we get there?"

"You're right." Sara agreed. "We've got to make some money fast. But how in the world can we do it?"

· Good News ·
from God's Word

Several years after Le's mother lost her husband, God brought new happiness into her life. Here's someone from the Bible who also found new happiness and love after great sadness.

Ruth Finds Love

FROM THE BOOK OF RUTH

Ruth was sad. She and her husband had loved each other very much. Then suddenly he became sick and died, leaving her a sad young widow.

Her mother-in-law Naomi was a widow too. "There's nothing in this country to live for now," Naomi told Ruth. "I'm going back to my old home in Israel."

"I'll go with you," Ruth said.

Now Naomi's little hometown didn't have any jobs suitable for Ruth. But the two women needed food to eat. There were farm fields all around the little town. So Ruth decided that maybe she could go work for a farmer. It would be a special kind of work called gleaning. The farmer

wouldn't pay her for working, but he would let her pick up extra grain from his fields and take it home.

The first field she came to was owned by a rich bachelor named Boaz [*bow-az*]. He was amazed to see how hard Ruth worked and how much she loved Naomi. He was also amazed at how beautiful Ruth was. Soon he fell in love with her.

She fell in love with him too. What a wedding it was! Everyone came from miles around to congratulate them. And they celebrated even more when God gave them a baby boy named Obed [*o-bed*]. Naomi was so happy for Ruth that she became Obed's babysitter. How glad everyone was that God had given Ruth a new loving family for her very own.

A Verse to Remember

"My purpose is that they may be encouraged in heart and united in love."

— Colossians 2:2

Bridesmaid Gown for Sam

Sam is trying on her new bridesmaid gown for Le's Mom's wedding. What color do you think it should be? Decorate the dress and put flowers in Sam's hair?

Learning about Love

You might enjoy asking your parents, your grandparents, or someone else how they met and fell in love. Then pray that God will lead you to the right person for you to marry in His own time, someone who loves God also, so that together you can have a Christian home.

The Greatest Show on Earth Puzzle

Add Secret Letter "O" for "open to loving others" to space 10 of the puzzle on pg. 27.

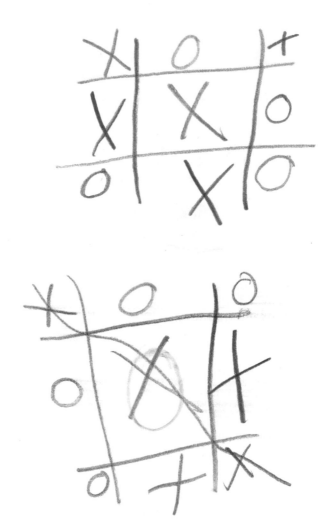

Chapter 12

Spray, Play, and Pray

"Yes," sighed Sonya. "What in the world will we do to earn money for the Fair?"

"I'm thinking, I'm thinking," Sam said. "Remember the Splash Party we had earlier this summer? What if we have a Splash-and-Spray party for kids in our backyard using our pools and sprinkler, and charge 50 cents each?"

"Also, some of the kids won't get to the Fair to see our puppet show," Jenna added. "Why don't we also put on our play just for kids in the neighborhood? We can charge 50 cents each for admission and give cookies and lemonade afterward."

Maria nodded. "So we can splash, spray, and play. I think we need to pray, too. But what if we only get five kids? We need at least $10 each for the Fair. What about also babysitting and dog walking? And selling some of the fudge we made?"

So they decided to make "Spray, Play, and Pray Day" posters and distribute them in their neighborhood and at church, telling about their Splash Party and Puppet Show. They also found babysitting and other jobs. They would do their best and leave the rest up to God.

Seven children turned up for the Splash Party. Seven children who were the PTs' brothers and sisters. "Oh, no!" moaned Maria. "They're all freebies. This is a bummer."

But when the neighbor children heard all the splashing and yelling, they soon started running over with their towels, swim clothes, and bright shining quarters. "Ten new kids," Sam reported happily.

"That's five whole dollars."

"Don't worry," La Toya retorted. "We're going to earn every penny of it."

Five of the children stayed for the puppet play. "Another two-fifty," counted up Sonya. "But it's still only seven dollars and fifty cents altogether. That's less than just one of us needs. Better keep on praying."

They did. Soon their phone starting ringing off the hook. Apparently Sam's mom had told everyone at the Paws and Pooches Animal Shelter about the PTs' "Spray, Play, and Pray Day." She'd also shared the news with the owner of the Four-Legged Friends pet store.

Soon they had enough dog walking jobs at $5 each to make their heads spin. For the next few hours they didn't even have time for lunch. Even Sonya got in the act with her wheelchair, with five dogs pulling her.  "This is like a chariot!" she laughed.

Sonya then counted up their money after all the dog walking. The PTs were up to $75. "Not quite enough," she decided.

"But I already have money for my own ticket," Brittany announced.

Sonya blushed. "Oh, I forgot. So do I. My Dad's paying for Little Red Wing and me."

"Then there's enough left over for Lilia and Angie, too," Sam cried. "Wow, is God good or what?"

"And just in time," Brittany added. "Because the County Fair is going to be here in just two days. I can hardly wait!"

· Good News · from God's Word

Because they wanted to do good for God, He helped the PTs figure out how to get the funds they needed. Long ago in Egypt, God helped two other people figure out how to do something good. Do you know what it was?

Pharaoh's Daughter
EXODUS 2:1-10

Long ago in Egypt all the kings were called "Pharaoh" [*fay-row*]. Each Pharaoh had absolute power over all the people in the land. At the time God's people, called the Hebrews or Israelites, were living in Egypt along with the Egyptians. They had come to Eygpt hundreds of years before when Joseph was second in command in the nation. The Pharaoh who knew Joseph was kind to God's people.

But as the years went by, new Pharaohs were born and came to power. Soon the Egyptians became jealous of the Israelites. "We'll make them our slaves," one of the Pharaohs decided.

So they did. They made the Israelites build pyramids and temples and roads and whatever the Pharaoh wanted. And they were very cruel to them. In fact, one day, Pharaoh gave new orders: kill all the baby Israelite boys!

Pharaoh had a daughter, a Princess. We don't know how old she was, or if she was married yet. She may have been an older teenager. But she heard about her father's order. How sad to kill innocent little boys. But she was helpless to change the law.

Now the Pharaoh's palace was right by the beautiful Nile River. Every morning the Princess and her friends liked to go down to the river and wade.

There were plants there near the bank that looked like cattails. They were called rushes or reeds. There were also fish and frogs and lots of birds. Everything was beautiful and peaceful.

But one morning the Princess saw something unusual in the water. "Look!" she said to her servants. "That looks like a basket. Could someone get it for me?"

So one of the young women waded over to the basket and brought it back to the Princess. When she opened it, guess what? There was a baby inside!

When the sun got in his eyes, the little baby woke up and began crying. "Poor little baby," cried the Princess. "He is so darling. This must be one of those Hebrew babies."

Just then a young girl popped out of the rushes. "Would you like me to find a babysitter for your new baby, Your Majesty?" she asked. The young girl was named Miriam. She was the baby's big sister.

Suddenly the Princess fell in love with that little baby. "Yes," she said, "find someone to take care of my baby for me. I'll pay her well."

And that's how the Princess adopted a little boy. She named him Moses. Miriam took baby

Moses home to her mother to care for until he was older. So everyone was happy—Miriam, her mother, and the Princess. God had helped them all.

A Verse to Remember

"Be openhanded toward your brothers and toward the poor and needy in your land."

— Deuteronomy 15:11

The Greatest Show on Earth Puzzle

Add the Secret Letter "S" for "seeking God's guidance" to space 4 of the puzzle on pg. 27.

When You Grow Up Word Search Puzzle

Here are a few career possibilities to choose from for your adult working life. You may end up with more than one choice. And there are many more we didn't have room to list! See how many of the listed careers you can find in this puzzle. Be sure to ask God to guide you so you can prepare to be just what He wants you to be. Remember, words can go left to right or right to left, and up to down or down to up. And letters can be used in more than one word.

Some possibilities for you:

Actor   Architect
Athlete   Business
Cop   Decorator
Designer   Engineering
Investigate   Medicine
Model   Mother
Music   Painting
Pilot   Plumber
Senator   Teacher
Vet   Write

Chapter 13

Break a Leg!

Petie ran inside waving the morning paper. "The Fair starts tomorrow!" he yelled. "Look at everything they're going to have."

He pointed to the front page pictures, all in full color. "This Daredevil Drop drops 100 feet. Look at these tractors for the tractor pull contest. And there's a Ferris wheel, sky ride, motocross, roller coaster, circus, even Chinese lion dancers."

Sam crowded over his shoulders to see. "Look at all the kids in the 4H tent. And there's a frog-jumping contest, a hotdog-eating contest, a petting barn, and lots of concerts, including the Rubber Band, and—"

Suddenly she stopped and squealed. "Petie! Look at that horse and rider," she shouted, pointing to one photo. "It's Ric and Gallant!"

Ric was proudly showing off Gallant's tricks. "Oh, I bet he wins first place," her little brother said. "It'll be amazing if we win anything."

Sam looked at the clock. "We won't if we don't get started. Today's the day to pull everything together—and hope it all works."

What a day that was! Everyone got together for their last puppet show and band practice. Then everything, including Sneezit, had to be packed up and hauled over to the

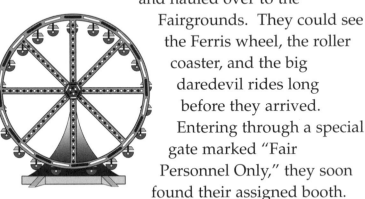

Fairgrounds. They could see the Ferris wheel, the roller coaster, and the big daredevil rides long before they arrived. Entering through a special gate marked "Fair Personnel Only," they soon found their assigned booth.

"Oh, good," Miss Kitty said. "It's near the front gate. That should get us lots of foot traffic."

Sara's big brother Tony grinned. "Then we better put our best foot forward, shouldn't we?" He held up a clown costume. "Granny B just finished making it for me. Hope it fits. I told her to make it plenty large so I'd have room to eat all the hot dogs and fudge I wanted. I'm getting awfully tired of eating burgers down at the Yum-Yum Palace."

After they arranged the puppet stage and folding chairs in their Youth Booth and decorated everything with banners and flags, they headed out to find Ric, Lilia, and their other friends who were bringing animals.

Ric was at the corral with Gallant. Everyone had to give the gentle horse a pat and a handful of hay. "I'm really excited," Ric said. "But Gallant and I haven't been a team for very long. I know he won't goof up. But what if *I* do?"

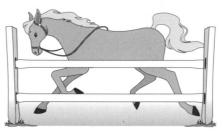

"You'll do just fine," Sonya assured him. "As they say in show business, 'Break a leg!'"

"Oooo," Sam cried. "Don't say that. That's the very last thing you want to happen to a horse. Especially to one as awesome as Gallant."

Mr. Silverhorse and his friends at McAfee Farms were sponsoring the 4H tent. His co-workers at Superservice Auto had arranged for transportation for all of them. Lilia Lancaster had already set up her stall in the 4H tent for her pet lamb, Cuddles. The farm dog, Pooch, was there, too. Lilia brought cages for her rooster and hen to use when they weren't performing. Also, all the kids had blankets for sleeping on the hay at night beside their pets.

Animals were everywhere—cows and goats and sheep and ducks and geese and hamsters and rabbits and more. The PTs petted them all, helped give them all fresh water and food, and cleaned up their cages and stalls. What fun they were having.

But they were also getting very tired and very hot and sweaty. Pretty soon Sam accused Sara of being more interested in the animals than in their puppet show. And Maria decided she didn't like her lines in the play and wanted them changed. And one of the big rubber bands they were going to use in the band for "harps" broke. And Beetle threatened to quit the band because he didn't have a good-enough music stand.

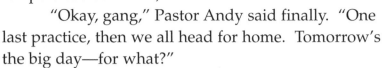

"Time out, everyone!" called Pastor Andy. "Let's have a hot dog and ice cream break. And a prayer-and-hug break, too."

After they sat in the shade and cooled down, tempers cooled down, too.

"Okay, gang," Pastor Andy said finally. "One last practice, then we all head for home. Tomorrow's the big day—for what?"

And everyone yelled, "For the greatest show on earth!"

"Yea!" Sonya said. "And since I'm not supposed to say, 'break a leg,' I'll just tell everyone to 'shake a leg.' And don't forget to set your alarm clock. It's time for the Fair!"

· Good News ·
from God's Word

We all love having friends. We all love being friends. But it's not always easy. Sometimes we say harsh words to each other we don't mean or do something that hurts a friend's feelings. Then we need to make things right and be a good friend again—like Claudia.

Blessing of Friends like Claudia
2 TIMOTHY 4:19-22

What if there were only one Ponytail Girl in the whole world? She could still be happy, but she might be very lonely. However, if she met some other girls and told them about Jesus and invited them to her church, and they became Christians, too, she wouldn't be lonely anymore. She would have friends.

When kids move to new schools where they don't know anyone, they can feel lonely. Life can be very hard. That's why it's so important to be friendly and kind to new students at school and new neighbors near your home. The Bible says we're to help them and show God's love to them.

As Paul traveled through many countries around Israel, he would have been very lonely without friends. But everywhere he went he made friends. Many times when he moved to a new country, his friends moved there too.

One of Paul's friends was young Timothy. Paul was always trying to encourage Timothy. That's why he wrote him two letters. They're both in our Bible, called 1st and 2nd Timothy. When Paul became a prisoner in Rome, Luke and other friends were with him. He encouraged Timothy to come visit him, too. He mentioned several other friends who were with him, including several men and a woman named Claudia.

We don't know any more about Claudia. Maybe she helped bring home-cooked meals to Paul or helped the poor. Maybe she sat in on Paul's Bible classes or taught one herself for the other women. What we do know is that she was Paul's friend and

Timothy's friend, too. God put her name in the Bible just for being a friend.

It's not always easy being a friend. Sometimes we quarrel and fuss at each other, just the way the PTs and their friends did on that long, hot day getting ready for the Fair. But our Heavenly Father can help us apologize, make up, and be glad for the friends He has given us.

He also wants us to be the kind of friends other girls can thank Him for.

A Verse to Remember

"I will be a Father to you,
and you will be my sons and daughters."
— 2 Corinthians 6:18

The Greatest Show
on Earth Puzzle

Add Secret Letter "T" for "turning things over to God" to space 9 of the puzzle on pg. 27.

Ric and Gallant

Ric Romero is putting his horse Gallant through his tricks. As you decorate them, think of some tricks they could perform. Do you have a special pet? Would you like your own horse, too?

Chapter 14

El Pollo Loco!!

Finally! The first day of the Fair and Sam felt like turning somersaults. The sky was clear, the sun was bright and the air was cooler than it had been for days. All the people loved that—and so did the animals.

Sam almost got dizzy watching the Ferris wheel and roller coaster sparkle in the sun. Bright flags fluttered in the breeze, voices blared over the loudspeakers, and the horses, cows, sheep, and goats all kept up a clamor. So did the eager people rushing in through the gates.

Kevin and Ryan filled lots of balloons to float at the top of the Youth Booth; their work looked almost like a rainbow. Granny B wheeled around in her wheelchair handing out puppet show tickets and fudge samples. It was perfect!

Then Pooch started barking at the parakeets, and the parakeets started squawking at Pooch. Cocky kept crowing every five minutes no matter what time it was. Sneezit became sick to his stomach and so did LaToya. By ten in the morning the kids had already run out of bottled water and Pastor Andy had to go buy more. Tony's clown costume ripped and his big red nose fell off. And some crows came by and started popping the balloons. Then some hungry ants tried to haul off the cookies and fudge.

"This is crazy!" Sam cried. "Everything's going wrong."

"Not everything," laughed Maria. "Look! Here comes Sonya with Little Red Wing and her dog, Chico."

Little Red Wing's long black hair pulled back at her neck. "She has a ponytail, too. I told her she'd fit right in," Sonya said.

Even though Sonya's friend was blind, her smile was as big as the Fair grounds. And when Miss Kitty heard her sing, she was thrilled. "You've got to sing at our concert," she insisted. "My friend Matty is arriving in town tomorrow. I know she'll love to hear you sing too."

Several families stopped by the Youth Booth and accepted tickets for the afternoon puppet show. The kids loved the fudge, but seemed more excited about the rides than about seeing a puppet show.

Sam and her friends gulped down some sandwiches and juice and got ready for the big afternoon. They made sure all the folding chairs were lined up neatly, found places for all the musicians, and got all the puppets ready for the play. Pastor Andy had rigged up some microphones and an amplifier so that passersby would be able to hear the play as well.

At last it was one o'clock. "Nobody's here," complained Brittany, looking around at the empty seats. So Pastor Andy grabbed the mic and called out, "Free puppet play! Free music! Free fudge and cookies and lemonade!"

Tony clowned around outside, juggling balls. Soon people started straggling in, including some kids Sam's age who just wanted something free to eat.

"And now," Tony announced, "may we present the Greatest Show on Earth!"

When the musicians took their seats—all wearing straw hats and playing everything from a washtub to a guitar to a big rubber band—the children began giggling. When they realized that Rocky and Cocky and Pooch and Sneezit and the parakeets were also part of the Rubber Band, they almost died laughing. And when they heard the songs, they stomped their feet and tried to sing along.

Because the music was being broadcast over the amplifiers, other Fair-goers heard it as well. Soon a large crowd had formed outside the booth. Some were taking pictures on their cell phones; others started recording the music.

Then Little Red Wing stood up to sing. People right away could see that she was blind, and they quickly quieted down to hear her sweet voice on "God Bless America." Afterwards, everyone clapped and cheered.

"And now," Tony announced, "the puppet show we promised you."

But before they could open the stage curtains, Cocky suddenly flapped his wings, flew out of the booth, and landed right on top of a man's head—and he happened to be a reporter from Channel 7.

"Cock-a-doodle-doo!" Cocky crowed, very proud of himself.

Oh, no! Now everything was ruined.

· Good News · from God's Word

The PTs' church isn't huge, but it's large enough for plenty of kids their age to attend. What if you attended a church so small it had no kids your age in it at all?

Home Churches

— COLOSSIANS 4:13-16

When you think of a church, you probably think of a building, don't you? It might be old, it might be new. It might be made of brick or stone or wood. It could be in the city or in the country. It could be very large or very small. Maybe it has a steeple and cross on top. But it is a very real place to go to—just like the Faith Church that the PTs attend.

But what if you didn't have any churches in your town? Where would you go to study God's Word? Where would you go to be with other Christians? What if there were too few of you to build your own church? Or what if building a church was against the law, as it is many places around the world? What would you do then?

As Paul and his friends traveled on missonary trips telling people about Jesus, many people believed and became Christians. There were no church buildings in their towns, but that didn't stop them

from having churches. They met in many places, including people's homes.

There were house churches back in New Testament times and there are still some today. They can never grow very large—most homes don't have room for too many people to meet together. And, unfortunately, some cities have laws against them. But such churches are a great way to study God's Word and have fellowship together, even if they're small.

And God will be with His people, just as if they were in the largest church building in the world.

A Verse to Remember

"And whatever you do, whether in word or deed, do it all in the name of the Lord Jesus, giving thanks to God the Father through him."

— **Colossians 3:17**

Fun at the Fair

Have you ever been to a County Fair or a State Fair? What did you like best about it? If you've never been to a real Fair yourself, think of some of the fun things about Fairs that you've learned from the PTs so far. Then think of all the other fun things there—hot dogs and  flower shows, craft and art exhibits, fried chicken, pig races, and all the rest. What would YOU like most to do at the Fair if you could go?

The Greatest Show on Earth Puzzle

Put Secret Letter "O" for "overcoming problems" in space 16 of the puzzle on pg. 27.

Fair Rhyme Time

See which words from the right side best finish the rhymes on the left.

1. Yes, it's time for our Fair to begin,
So buy a ticket and walk right

_____ .

A. treat

2. I like to shout and shiver and squeal,
When I take a ride on the

_____ .

B. cow

3. The horses run and soon they're back,
As we watch them race around the

_____ .

C. display

4. Hot dogs and corn on the cob to eat,
With ice cream as a special

_____ .

D. in

5. Pies and paintings the judges judge,
Plus pickles and pumpkins, tomatoes,
and _____ .

E. Fair

6. Who raised the best chickens? Who
raised the best sow? Who raised the best
rabbits? Who raised the best

_____ ?

F. Ferris wheel

7. We'll enjoy rides and games all the day,
And then at night a fine fireworks

_____ .

G. track

8. There's nothing that can even compare,
To spending the day at a wonderful

_____ !

H. fudge

Chapter 15

Say, "Cheese!"

Lilia ran after Cocky. Oh, no! This was a television reporter. And his cameraman was right behind him. Everything was being filmed.

"Oh, sir," she apologized to the man. "I'm so sorry. Cocky's never done anything like that before. Bad bird," she scolded.

But the rooster just cuddled up to the reporter's shoulder. Then he leaned over and rubbed his head against the camera. "Awwwk!" he crowed.

All the children screamed with delight. "He wants his picture taken," little Lolita yelled.

"Well, he's getting his wish, isn't he?" the cameraman laughed.

By that time a huge crowd had gathered around the Youth Booth. "It's time for our puppet show," Pastor Andy announced. "If you can't stay to see it, come back at two or three this afternoon. We'll have three showings today. We'll also be here Saturday and Sunday afternoons."

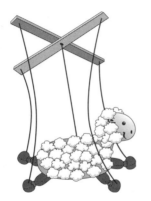

Then they put on the play. There were some funny parts, like the sheep cracking jokes before the angels came. But mostly everything was serious.

At the end Pastor Andy told the children why Jesus had come into the world as a baby so long ago. "God loves you," he said. "He wants you to love Him, too, and to be His child."

Sam's little cousin Suzie stood up with a big grin. "Yes," she said. "That's what I did. And everyone else in the whole world should do it too. Just hold up your hand and say yes to God."

And four children did.

Sam's looked around to see if the reporter was still there. He wasn't. But it didn't make any difference. God was there. And so were the angels.

Suddenly everything was worth it, including silly old Cocky.

After that audience left, Miss Kitty came by—twice. Or at least that's what it looked like. Sam had to rub her eyes to make sure she wasn't seeing double.

"Hi, everyone," their teacher called. "This is my friend Matty Hawkins. Her plane from Ohio just arrived in Summer City a couple of hours ago. I can't wait for you all to meet her."

Just then someone rode by on a horse. Ric and Gallant had arrived.

Ric looked very serious. "Everyone keep me in your prayers, please," he asked. "The trick riding competition starts at five o'clock sharp! And for some reason, Gallant is getting very, very nervous."

· Good News · from God's Word

Working the booths at the Fair and putting on the puppet show wasn't easy, but the PTs and their friends did it because they loved God. Here's a Bible story about a woman who also loved God and wanted to help Him— and help Paul, too.

Rufus' Mother Helps Paul

ROMANS 16:13

Aren't mothers wonderful? But not everyone has a mother. Some children, like Miss Kitty and Little Red Wing, are orphans whose mothers have gone to be with Jesus.

But loving women can act like mothers to orphans, helping them, comforting them, advising them, hugging them. That's the way Ma Jones cared for Miss Kitty and for all the other children at their orphanage. That's the way Sarah in the Old Testament cared for her motherless nephew Lot.

And that's how Rufus' mother cared for Paul. In fact, Paul tells us that she had "been a mother to me, too." We don't know in what ways she acted motherly to him. Maybe she cooked his favorite food when he was in town. Maybe she sent him "CARE" packages when he was traveling or in prison. Maybe she gave him advice and comfort when he was lonely.

Has someone in your life, besides your own mother, been like a mother to you? Maybe it was an aunt, a grandmother, a teacher, a school counselor, or even a neighbor. Maybe it was your Sunday school or VBS teacher. If so, thank God for her. And write or call her to thank her, too.

And, remember, when you grow up, *you* can be a good friend like that, not just to your own children, but to all the children you know.

A Verse to Remember

"Salvation is found in no one else,
for there is no other name under heaven
given to men by which we must be saved."

— *Acts 4:12*

The Greatest Show on Earth Puzzle

Add Secret Letter "Y" for "yearning to see decisions for Christ" to space 15 of the puzzle on page 27.

Telling Someone Thank You

Miss Matty wanted to call her old friend, Miss Kitty. But she had a hard time getting her call through. See if you can untangle these wires and help her make the right connection.

Chapter 16

Horse of a Different Color

After the puppet play and concert, the Zone 56ers served all their guests cookies and fudge and lemonade. Then they cleaned up their Fair booth and prepared to enjoy the evening.

"Miss Kitty," Sam said, "now that you and Miss Matty finally got together, have you solved the mystery of your past?"

Their teacher laughed. "Well, not totally. Just

141

that we were indeed both in the same spot at the same time when we were little, and we both liked each other. And looked like each other. You know, back in those days they didn't always keep good records of orphans. And the Mississippi orphanage went out of business long ago. Why, we could even be related and not know it."

"But you are going to keep looking into it, aren't you?"

"Of course, dear. And now, let's all look into what else is going on at this Fair."

Their first stop was the Craft and Cooking Tent. LaToya's mom's sweet potato pie was on exhibit there and three of Granny B's quilts. Plus the largest pumpkin Sam had ever seen in her life. The Painting and Photo Tent included paintings done by Sara's parents and Angie's cartoons and dog portraits.

LaToya won a second prize in gymnastics and Beetle won honorable mention for his skateboarding routine. Suddenly Sam remembered, "The Trick Riding competition—it starts in just five minutes!"

They just reached the Grandstand in time. One girl rode her horse while wearing a ballerina's tutu. She even stood up on the saddle. "Oooo, she's good," Brittany said.

One rider was dressed up like a clown, with a red nose like the one Tony had worn that afternoon. He kept pretending to fall off. Finally the horse just sat down and pretended to give up.

Another rider was dressed like a cowboy, doing fancy lariat tricks.

Then it was Ric's turn. When he rode in, everyone gasped in amazement. For instead of a saddle, he sat on a beautiful blanket of red, white, and blue, with one gold cross on each side and long tassels at each corner. Some people clapped while others frowned. *Why in the world would a serious trick rider sit on something that gaudy?* they wondered.

Sam sat down by her Aunt Caitlin and little cousin Suzie. "Lolita and I made that blanket for him," Suzie announced. "My mom and Lolita's mom helped too. We did it because we love Gallant. So Ric said he'd put it on Gallant just for us. And he did."

When Ric went into his routine, jeers soon turned to cheers. He was really good, and so was Gallant. If the horse was nervous, it didn't even show. If fact, he won a blue ribbon!

Then it was time for games and rides and lots and lots to eat. That night they watched a country-western concert, then oohed and aahed over wonderful fireworks.

At last it was time to head home. Sam could hardly wait to pull on her 'jammies and plop into bed. But her Dad decided to watch the late news on the TV. Suddenly he called, "Sam! Petie! Come quick! You won't believe what I see on Channel 7!"

· Good News · from God's Word

The PTs found a lot of blessings at the Fair, didn't they? Someone else found a lot of blessings long ago out in the open air by the river—a woman named Lydia!

Lydia's Blessings

ACTS 16:11-15

"Paul," God said. "I want you to go to the country of Macedonia [mass-uh-dough-knee-uh] and tell them about Jesus."

"But I don't know anyone there," Paul explained.

Then God sent him a vision of a man begging Paul for help. "Come over to Macedonia and help us," the man said. So then Paul was convinced, and he and his friends sailed to this new country.

Finally they reached the city of Philippi [fill-ih-pie]. Was this where the man lived that Paul saw in his vision? There weren't any churches or synagogues

in this city. Most people there were pagans.

On the Sabbath, Paul and his friends went to the river outside of the city. Some Jewish women were praying there. Paul and his friends sat down with them and began telling them about Jesus. How thrilled the women were!

One of the women was a rich merchant named Lydia. She was so excited to hear about Jesus that she became a Christian right then. Paul baptized her. When her family heard about Jesus, they all became Christians too. So Paul baptized them, too.

"Now that we are all Christians," Lydia said, "why don't all of you come stay at my house? We can all study the Bible together there."

So the first Christians in Philippi weren't men, after all, but women. But because Paul was faithful in telling the Gospel, the women believed. And soon many men believed, too.

What a blessing Paul and his friends were to everyone. And the new Christians were just as much a blessing to Paul.

A Verse to Remember

"A faithful man will be richly blessed."

— **Proverbs 28:20**

The Greatest Show on Earth Puzzle

Put Secret Letter "V" for "very grateful for God's blessings" in space 12 of the puzzle on pg. 27. Just two more missing letters to fill in. Have you figured out the puzzle yet?

Granny B's Blessings Quilt

Here's one of the quilts Granny B entered in the County Fair. To see its message, use one color to fill in all the areas that contain dots. Then color the other areas using different colors.

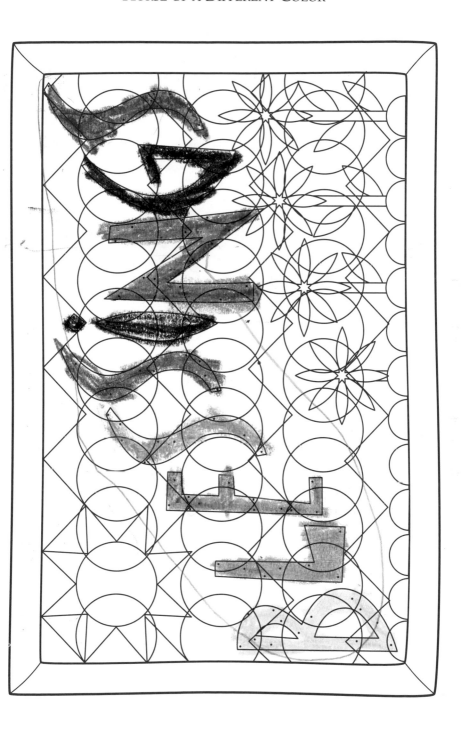

Chapter 17

Surprise, Surprise!

Sam threw on her robe and ran into the living room. "I-i-ee!" she screamed. "It's us!"

Petie stumbled out of his room, rubbing his eyes. "Did someone yell, 'Fire'?" he asked with a yawn.

"No, Petie, look at the TV! That's our band,

and that's our puppet show. And there's Cocky on top of the reporter's head. And look at Tony in his clown suit. And Little Red Wing singing."

"I see both Miss Kittys," her little brother joked. "And Suzie and Granny B. Hey, we're famous."

Someone else must have thought so, too. The next morning, Sam got a phone call from Miss Kitty. "Guess what? Pastor Andy just called me because the Fair Director just called him.

The Director wants us to move our show from the Youth Booth to the Sunset Stage for today and tomorrow. Instead of 20 seats, we'll have 200!"

"I bet it's because we were on TV," Sam said. "Did you see the news program last night?"

"Yes. And it's also on the news this morning and in today's paper. And since today is Saturday, we'll probably get a lot more people there. So we'll need a lot more lemonade and fudge."

Now was time to ask the question Sam had been dying to ask. "Miss Kitty, do you and Miss Matty know any more about your past than you did before she came to visit?"

"Thank you for asking. Not yet. But I'm taking her to meet Ma Jones at the Whispering Pines Nursing Home this morning. Maybe she can give us some clues. But even if she can't, I know she'll love meeting Matty. I already feel as if I've known Matty all my life."

Soon the PTs and family and friends were making pan after pan of fudge. They had to buy more paper cups and napkins, too, plus make a big sign to put at the Youth Booth to direct people across the walk to the Sunset Stage. They also made two big signs to put up on the stage when it was their time to perform. Also, Pastor Andy bought a lot of children's Gospel tracts to distribute, and he made some little cards on his computer with their church's picture, phone number, address, and a welcome from Pastor McConahan. On the back were more welcomes written in Spanish and Vietnamese.

Not everything went exactly the way they planned. Tony was called in early to work at the Yum-Yum Palace, so Beetle Boxer took his place. They had a hard time getting their puppet stage up on the big Sunset Stage. Some of the fudge was too soft to cut, so they had to keep it in a cooler until it hardened.

When the Rubber Band set up their music stands on the stage, someone turned a fan on and blew all the sheet music away. Rocky and Cocky flew up onto the tent rafters and didn't want to come down. Miss Kitty and Miss Matty didn't get there until the last minute, so Sam didn't get to ask her about their get-together with Ma Jones.

But finally everyone got together and prayed that they could do a good job. "Let this not be about us, Lord," Ryan prayed, "but about You."

"Yes," added Sara. "Help the children and their families see your love for them and be filled with the desire to love You back."

The show went very well—several children even raised their hands afterwards to talk to someone from the play about Jesus. And so did three grown-ups. Yes, God was really blessing everyone.

Afer the show, everyone had time to sit down and eat some pizza and watermelon.

"Now," Sam said, "Miss Kitty, how did your meeting with Ma Jones go?"

Their teacher and her friend looked at each other. "Wonderful, Sam," Miss Matty said. "In fact, better than wonderful."

"You see," Miss Kitty explained, "when Ma Jones saw both of us together, she almost passed

out—the way I almost did when I saw that old picture of Matty and me together. When she could finally speak, she gasped, 'It's true then. The story about the Kotter twins is really true.'"

Miss Matty continued the tale. "Then she had one of the nurses get a suitcase for her out of the Whispering Pines storeroom. It was just full of old letters and pictures and forms and an old Bible. Then she pulled out an old torn envelope marked, 'For the Kotter twins.'"

"She said that I was the only little Kotter girl she ever knew," Miss Kitty added. "So she didn't know what to do with the envelope. So all those years it was filed away at the orphanage, until the orphanage closed down. Then because she didn't know what else to do with it, she took it with her."

"Did you open it?" everyone shouted at once.

Now their teacher was crying. "Yes," she said, "and guess what? It held a newspaper clipping from a little Mississippi paper about Dr. John and Mrs. Sue Kotter having twin girls, Matty and Kitty. And another article about how our parents were killed in a boating accident. Since we didn't have any other relatives the authorities could find, we were both sent to the orphanage."

"I was adopted and Kitty wasn't," Matty explained. "So she went on to the orphanage in Tennessee by herself. We were both very young. That's why it's hard for us to remember it all. But tomorrow morning I'm calling my adopted parents. They're wonderful people. And I'm dying for them to meet my new sister. She's the greatest."

At that, all the girls jumped up and hugged them both. What an amazing surprise! Would there be an even bigger one tomorrow?

· Good News ·
from God's Word

What a great day at the Fair! Someone else long ago had a very special great day, too—a day for music and dancing and praising God.

Job's Daughters Rejoice

THE BOOK OF JOB

Job [*jobe*] lived long, long ago. He lived not in Israel but in the Land of Uz. This was east of the Jordan River, in the area where the country of Jordan is today.

He and his wife were very happy and very wealthy. They owned thousands of animals, had vast amounts of farmland, and employed many people to help them. Indeed, he was called "the greatest man among all the people of the East" (meaning all those who lived east of the Jordan River.)

It was nice to be rich. But that's not why Job and his wife were happy. They were happy because they loved and worshipped God and because God had blessed them with a large family—three girls and seven boys.

Then one day their whole world fell apart. All their animals were killed. So were their servants. And so were all their now-grown up children. And it all happened on the very same day. Job even became very sick.

Some of Job's friends came to visit him. "You obviously did something very bad to make God punish you," they said. "You'd better ask God to forgive you."

"But I didn't do anything very bad," Job cried. "I love God! And I trust Him no matter what."

God knew Job loved him. Soon, God healed Job and blessed him with even more possessions than before. Instead of 7,000 sheep, he soon had 14,000. Instead of 3,000 camels, God gave him 6,000. And instead of 500 donkeys and 500 yoke of oxen, he had 1,000 of each.

Best of all, God gave Job and his wife ten more children–seven more boys and three more girls. His new daughters were named Jemimah, Keziah, and Keren-Happuch.

Little Jemimah, Keziah, and Karen knew their parents loved them very much. Their mother and father taught them to love God, too. And when they grew up, they were considered the most beautiful young women in their land.

Even though Job and his wife had known a lot of sorrow, they now rested in God's love and rejoiced at all His blessings.

A Verse to Remember

"O Lord, my Lord, how majestic is your name in all the earth!"
— **Psalm 8:9**

The Greatest Show on Earth Puzzle

Put Secret Letter "O" for "overcoming problems with God's help" in space 6 of the puzzle on pg. 27. Just one more Secret Letter to go!

The Twinkle Twins

Here are Miss Kitty and Miss Matty (known as the "Twinkle Twins" back then) when they were very young. Decide which girl below is Kitty and which is Matty. Decorate their picture.

#
Brittany
Sam
Le
Latya
Maria

Chapter 18

Bubbles of Blessing

"And guess what else?" Miss Kitty laughed. "I heard from Miss Temple that Madison Middle School needs a girls' gym teacher for this year. Guess what Matty teaches?"

"P.E.!" everyone shouted at once.

"So that's why she's so good at snorkeling,"

Brittany decided. "But we can't snorkel in our cornfields."

Miss Kitty's sister laughed. "No, but we can play volleyball and basketball and soccer and all the rest. Anyway, I'm going to stop by Madison on Monday to put in my application before I leave."

Basketball? Yea! Sam and her pals loved basketball—even Sonya with her wheelchair team.

"And my apartment's big enough for a roommate," Miss Kitty added. "Boy, it's been a long time since we roomed together, hasn't it, Matty? Not since we were four years old."

Sunday morning it seemed strange to be back in church instead of at the Fair. Everyone there wanted to meet Miss Matty. She especially hit it off with Sonya's dad, Mr. Silverhorse. And when Sonya's new friend, Little Red Wing, sang "Amazing Grace" for a solo, everyone sniffled and whispered, "Isn't that beautiful?"

"You know, Miss Kitty," Sonya said, "you now have a new sister. And I may soon have a new sister, too. Wouldn't that be awesome?"

"Just like I'm soon going to have new brothers," Le added. "Wow, how are we going to keep them all straight?"

After church, there was barely time for everyone to grab something to eat, change clothes, and head over to the Fair. Today was the very last day.

Today's special guests were all Lilia's friends whose parents worked for the McAfee Farms. Maria's mother translated for those who needed help. As a special treat, Angie's father wore his military uniform. Because he'd lost one of his hands, when he led everyone in saluting the flag, the hand he saluted with was his new artificial one made of metal.

But Angie had never been prouder of him. Her mother, who was feeling much better these days, was proud of him, too. She couldn't stop squeezing Angie's hand.

The 56ers ran out of fudge and lemonade long before they ran out of children wanting to hear their band and see their play. So Pastor Andy handed out little bottles of soap bubble liquid instead. He called them "Bubbles of Blessings."

At the end of the performance, everyone stood up on stage for the curtain call. Sam held Miss Kitty's hand tight. But what was this? She felt something rough and sharp on one of Miss Kitty's fingers. She almost wanted to jerk her hand away.

But she waited till everyone finished clapping. Then she pulled away and glanced at her teacher's hand. Was that a sparkle?

"Miss Kitty!" she cried. "Is that an engagement ring?"

Suddenly Pastor Andy was hugging them both. "It sure is," he said. "Miss Kotter has made me the happiest man on earth."

The PTs' teacher smiled. "He asked me to marry him when we were both in Peru on our missions trip. So guess what I said?"

"YES!" all the PTs squealed.

All but Sonya.

Wait a minute! she said to herself. *I thought God was going to have Miss Kitty marry my dad.*

And then she saw her father smiling at Miss Kitty's sister. So she smiled, too. *Well, well, God, You sure do work in mysterious ways. I don't know what Your plans are. But they're sure to be great.*

"A toast to Pastor Andy and Miss Kitty!" Mr. Silverhorse said. By now the lemonade and bottled

water was all gone, too. There was nothing left to make a toast with except the empty pink soap bubble bottles.

So everyone grabbed them and held them up. "Thank You, God," Pastor Andy said, "for all your blessings. Amen." Then, "And now, everyone, let's go find some more of that watermelon."

And they did. Everyone gobbled some down, even Rocky and Cocky and Pooch.

But not Sneezit. He insisted on a hot dog with lots of mustard.

But hold the relish, thank you very much!

· Good News ·
from God's Word

God can use anyone to carry out His plans. He used Moses' older sister Miriam when she was a little girl and again as an old woman.

When Miriam Sang for Joy
EXODUS 14:21-15:21

For 400 years God's people had lived in Egypt. At first life there was good. Then they became slaves. Life was hard.

But God had a plan to return His people to Israel. He also had the right person to help carry out this plan: Moses. When Moses was born, Egypt's ruler, Pharaoh [*fay-row*], told the Jewish women to kill their baby boys. Instead, Miriam helped her mother to save little Moses, who was soon adopted by an Egyptian Princess.

Moses grew up and moved away. He married and grew old. His big sister Miriam grew old, too. But God wasn't through using them.

One day, God called Moses to come back to Egypt. There God did miracles to convince Pharaoh to "let My people go." Finally Pharaoh told them they could go. So off they marched.

Then Pharaoh changed his mind. By now God's people were facing the Red Sea. This was the shallow end of the sea, but it was way too deep for anyone to cross without drowning.

"Don't worry," Moses told the people. "God will help us cross it safely."

And God did. He sent a great wind that blew and blew and blew a path right through the water. All the people crossed over on the bottom of the sea without ever getting wet.

"After them!" cried Pharaoh. But just then God released all of the water and it came rushing back. Pharaoh and his men drowned. And all God's people were safe.

How they rejoiced! God helped Moses write a beautiful song of praise. Moses taught it to the people and they all sang it together.

Moses' sister Miriam was a musician, too. Playing a tambourine, she led all the women in singing, dancing and praising the Lord, even though she was very old.

See, we're never too old or too young for God to use. How does God want to use YOU?

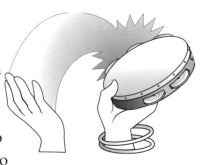

A Verse to Remember

"Consider the blameless, observe the upright;
there is a future for the man of peace."

— **Psalm 37:37**

Those I Love

Write down the names of your parents, brothers and sisters, grandparents, and other relatives. Also list others you love, such as your best friend, your pastor, or a teacher. Thank God for them all. And remember to pray for them.

_____

_____

_____

_____

_____

_____

The Greatest Show on Earth Puzzle

Now it's time to put "E" for "excited about God's plans" in space 13 of the puzzle on pg. 27. Now you're finished! Can you think of someone YOU can show and tell God's love to this week?

Heart to Heart

See how many of the hearts in this puzzle you can find. You can color them all red or mix in pink and leave some white. Give this to someone special as a reminder of your love for them.

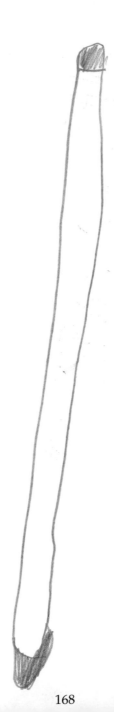

Extra Stuff

The following pages contain bonus Ponytail Girls activities and information especially for you. In this section you will find information on forming your own Ponytail Girls Club, including how to make membership cards.

The Ponytail Girls Club

Would you like to be a part of a Ponytail Girls Club? You can be a PT by yourself, of course. But it's much more fun if one of your friends joins with you. Or even five or six of them. There is no cost. You can read the Ponytail Girls stories together, do the puzzles and other activities, study the Bible stories, and learn the Bible verses.

If your friends have their own Ponytail Girls books, you can all write in your copies at the same time. Arrange a regular meeting time and place, and plan to do special things together, just like the PTs do in the stories: such things as shopping, Bible study, homework, or helping others.

Create membership cards similar to the ones on the following page and give one to each PT in your group.

Membership Cards

Give one membership card to each member of your Ponytail Girls club. Be sure to put your membership card in your wallet or another special place for safekeeping.

_____

is a member in good standing of
The Ponytail Girls Club.

_____
Signature

_____
Date

_____

is a member in good standing of
The Ponytail Girls Club.

_____
Signature

_____
Date

Do You Have Two Birthdays?

Being "born again" means becoming a new person through faith in Christ. You may look the same on the outside. You may even act the same, at first. But as you ask God daily to help you and as you try to live for Him, you will become more and more like Jesus. What a wonderful way to be! You'll even spend eternity with Him in heaven.

If you've already made that decision, praise the Lord! Aren't you glad? But if you haven't yet, this is a great time to do so. Don't think that you need to wait until you are older. You are at a perfect age to become a Christian. That way you'll have Jesus with you every single day, right on through middle school, high school, and beyond. Here's what to do if you're ready to make such a decision right now:

Get away to a quiet place where you will not be disturbed. Tell God you're sorry for all your sins. You can say it out loud or to yourself. God "hears" you either way. Thank Him for loving you so much that He gave His Son, Jesus, to die for you. Believe in Jesus as your Savior from sin. Ask Him to come into your heart and life and make you all new. Then praise Him for doing so.

If you just prayed that prayer now, sign and date the certificate below. Write that same information inside your Bible.

I made my decision for Christ today

signed: _____

Now tell someone, like your parents, pastor, or Sunday school teacher the Good News about what just happened to you.

Bible Verses to Remember and Share

These are the Bible verses the PTs studied throughout this book. Copy them onto pretty paper and learn them. Share your favorites with someone else!

*"Now, our God, we give you thanks,
and praise your glorious name."*
— 1 Chronicles 29:13

"Let everything that has breath praise the Lord."
— Psalm 150:6

"He has made everything beautiful in its time."
— Ecclesiastes 3:11

*"You will receive power when the Holy Spirit comes
on you; and you will be my witnesses."*
— Acts 1:8

*"Never be lacking in zeal, but keep your spiritual
fervor, serving the Lord."*
— Romans 12:11

"Do not be overcome by evil,
but overcome evil with good."
— Romans 12:21

"You are the light of the world."
— Matthew 5:14

"Always be prepared to give an answer
to everyone who asks you to give the reason
for the hope that you have."
— 1 Peter 3:15

"Love is patient, love is kind. It does not envy, it does
not boast, it is not proud."
— 1 Corinthians 13:4

"We have different gifts,
according to the grace given us."
— Romans 12:6

"My purpose is that they may be encouraged in heart
and united in love."
— Colossians 2:2

"Be openhanded toward your brothers and toward the
poor and needy in your land."
— Deuteronomy 15:11

"I will be a Father to you,
and you will be my sons and daughters."
— 2 Corinthians 6:18

"And whatever you do, whether in word or deed,
do it all in the name of the Lord Jesus,
giving thanks to God the Father through him."
— Colossians 3:17

"Salvation is found in no one else,
for there is no other name under heaven given to men
by which we must be saved."
— Acts 4:12

"A faithful man will be richly blessed."
— Proverbs 28:20

"O Lord, our Lord,
how majestic is your name in all the earth!"
— Psalm 8:9

"Consider the blameless, observe the upright;
there is a future for the man of peace."
— Psalm 37:37

Glossary (glos/ə rē)

Boaz [bow-az]
El pollo loco [el poy-yo loe-coe]:
Spanish phrase meaning, "the crazy chicken"
Goliath [go-lie-uth]
Herodias [hair-oh-dee-us]
Herod Antipas [hair-ud an-tih-pus]
Jemimah [jeh-my-muh]
Job [jobe]
Keren-Happuch [care-in hap-puck]
Keziah [kee-zee-uh]
Macedonia [mass-uh-dough-knee-uh]
Nebuchadnezzar [neb-u-chad-nez-zar]
Nehemiah [nee-he-my-ah]
Nympha [nim-fuh]
Obed [o-bed]
papier-mâché [pay-per muh-shay]
Pharaoh [fay-row]
Philippi [fill-ih-pie]
Philistine [fill-iss-teen]
Salome [sol-uh-may]
Sychar [sigh-car]
Zebedee [zeh-buh-dee]

Answers to Puzzles

Chapter 1
*The Greatest Show
on Earth Puzzle, page 27*

The Greatest Show on Earth

GOD'S LOVE
1 2 3 4 5 6 7 8

TO
9 10

EVERYONE
11 12 13 14 15 16 17 18

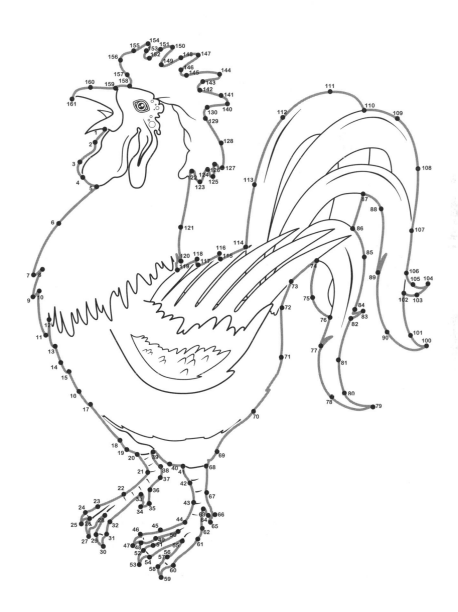

Chapter 3
It's a Zoo Out There!, page 47
Answers: 1-F, 2-J, 3-L, 4-H, 5-K, 6-A, 7-I, 8-D, 9-G,
10-B, 11-E, 12-C

Chapter 4
How to Share the Gospel, page 55
Answers:

• God loves you

• Jesus is God's Son

• Jesus died for you

• He rose from the dead

• Pray and ask Him to be your savior

Chapter 5
Searching for David!, page 63

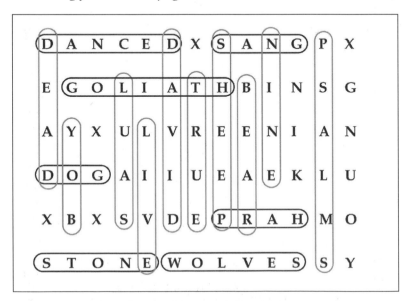

Chapter 8

The A-Maze-ing Skate Park!, page 87

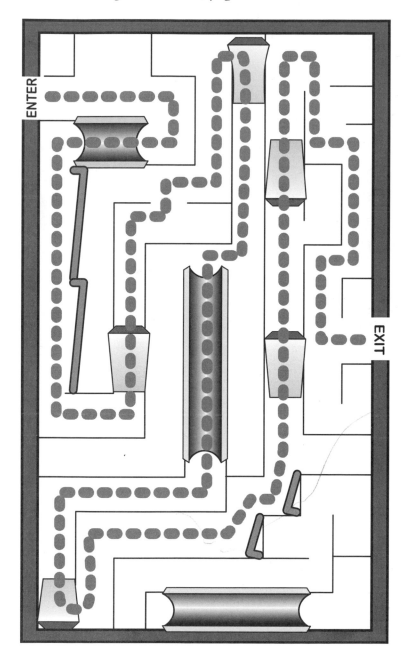

Chapter 9
Who's Who, page 95

Answers: 1-O, 2-F, 3-I, 4-K, 5-A, 6-B, 7-N, 8-L, 9-C, 10-M, 11-D, 12-H, 13-J, 14-G, 15-E

Chapter 12
When You Grow Up Word Search Puzzle, page 118

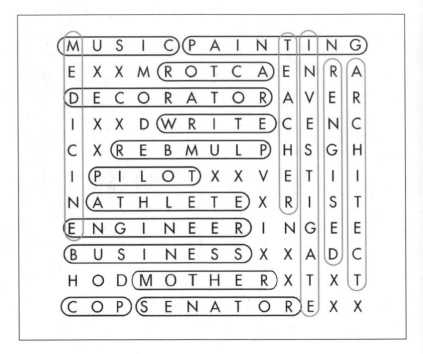

Chapter 14
Fair Rhyme Time, page 134

Answers: 1-D, 2-F, 3-G, 4-A, 5-H, 6-B, 7-C, 8-E

Chapter 16
Granny B's Blessings Quilt, pages 146-147

Chapter 18
Heart to Heart,
page 166
Answer at right.

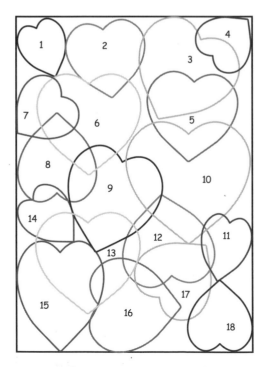